YOUNG WITCHES
& WARLOCKS

Anthologies edited by Isaac Asimov,
Martin H. Greenberg, and Charles G. Waugh:

YOUNG MUTANTS

YOUNG EXTRATERRESTRIALS

YOUNG MONSTERS

YOUNG GHOSTS

YOUNG STAR TRAVELERS

YOUNG WITCHES & WARLOCKS

EDITED BY ISAAC ASIMOV,
MARTIN H. GREENBERG, & CHARLES G. WAUGH

1979

HARPER & ROW, PUBLISHERS

Library of Congress Cataloging-in-Publication Data
Young witches & warlocks.

Summary: Ten short stories by a variety of authors
about young practitioners of witchcraft.
   1. Witchcraft—Fiction.   2. Short stories, American.
3. Short stories, English.   [1. Witchcraft—Fiction.
2. Short stories]   I. Asimov, Isaac, 1920–
II. Greenberg, Martin Harry.   III. Waugh, Charles G.
IV. Title: Young witches and warlocks.
PZ5.Y853 1987   [Fic]   85–45849
ISBN 0–06–020183–5
ISBN 0–06–020184–3 (lib. bdg.)

Acknowledgments

"The April Witch" by Ray Bradbury. Copyright 1952 by the Curtis Publishing Co.; renewed © 1980 by Ray Bradbury. Reprinted by permission of Don Congdon Associates, Inc. Copyright 1953 by Story Parade, Inc.

"Witch Girl" by Elizabeth Coatsworth. Reprinted by permission of the author. All rights reserved.

"The Wonderful Day" by Robert Arthur. Copyright 1940; renewed © 1968 by Robert Arthur. Reprinted by permission of the Scott Meredith Literary Agency, Inc., 845 Third Avenue, New York, N.Y. 10022.

"With Four Lean Hounds" by Pat Murphy. Copyright © 1984 by Pat Murphy. Reprinted by permission of the author.

"Mistress Sary" by William Tenn. Copyright 1947; renewed © 1975 by Phil Klass; reprinted by permission of the author and his agent Virginia Kidd.

"Teragram" by Evelyn E. Smith. Copyright © 1955 by King-Size Publications, Inc. Reprinted by permission of Henry Morrison, Inc.

"Stevie and The Dark" by Zenna Henderson. Copyright 1952 by Zenna Henderson. Reprinted by permission of Curtis Brown, Ltd.

"A Message from Charity" by William M. Lee. Copyright © 1967 by Mercury Press, Inc. From *The Magazine of Fantasy and Science Fiction*. Reprinted by permission of the agents for the author's Estate, the Scott Meredith Literary Agency, Inc., 845 Third Avenue, New York, N.Y. 10022.

"The Entrance Exam" by Mary Carey. Copyright © 1976 by Rand McNally and Company, Inc. Reprinted by permission of Macmillan Publishing pany.

Contents

Isaac Asimov

How Exciting!

We can do a great many marvelous things these days.
If we want to travel very quickly, all we have to do
is get into a plane and it will speed us through the air
at hundreds of miles an hour. A rocket ship will take
us to the moon at thousands of miles an hour.

If there is a marriage ceremony in London we want
to watch, we just turn on our television and there it
is right on the screen before our eyes.

We can walk toward a door, and it will open for us
even before we reach it. We don't need to do any
climbing if we want to get to the top of a tall building.
We just step into an elevator and it will whisk us
upward. It will take us down again, too.

We can press a button and a whole room lights up.
We can press another and cool air will begin to cir-

culate in summer (or warm air in winter). We turn a faucet and have all the cold water—or hot water—that we want. A microwave oven will heat our dinner in minutes.

We can sit at a word processor (as I am doing right now) and press certain typewriter keys, and paragraphs of writing appear on the screen. Press a few other keys and the writing will be automatically printed onto paper.

Yet none of this is particularly exciting. We know how it's done, or if we don't, we know that someone else knows how it's done. We also know that it will always work. If we want to turn on the light, we flick a switch. The lights will turn on no matter who flicks it. A baby can flick it and get light.

We also know that it's done by the use of energy. The lights burn because there is electricity coming into the house. The energy of electricity also runs the television set. The energy of burning gasoline drives automobiles and airplanes.

How dull!

There was a time, though, when people didn't know the power of electricity or burning gasoline. They didn't even know what energy was, or the way in which it had to be used in order to make things work. They didn't know that the universe was run by energy undergoing changes in accordance with what we call "the laws of nature," and that these laws of nature couldn't be changed.

In older times, people had no idea how the universe worked. They thought that it must be under the control of invisible and very powerful entities called gods or demons or any of many other names.

After all, we can water our gardens with sprinkling cans, for instance, so when it rained, wasn't that just some huge invisible rain-god watering the whole earth with an enormous sprinkling can? We can puff with our lungs and blow a feather through the air. When a huge storm wind came and blew down houses and trees, was that not some enormous storm-god blowing far more powerfully than we can? We light a fire on the hearth to warm the house. Was not the sun a huge fire lit by a sun-god in order to warm the whole earth?

If that were so,· and if gods or demons controlled the universe, then human beings might, in their turn, control the universe by dealing with those gods or demons. Human beings might pray and beg the gods and demons to do something kind and useful—make it rain, for instance, when rain was needed. Or they could threaten the gods and demons somehow, or learn how to force them into human service.

It was easy to imagine that some very wise human beings would learn special ways of forcing the gods and demons into service. There might be certain words and phrases that would do it, or certain motions of the hands, or certain magical objects.

However it was done, the people who knew these secrets could then use divine or demonic power to do amazing things. They could fly through the air, they could see things at a distance, they could foretell the future, they could change a prince into a frog or vice versa. . . .

Now *that's* exciting.

For one thing, it's secret. Only a few people would know how it was done and be able to do it. They were called witches or warlocks, depending on whether they were women or men. They were considered powerful and frightening, because if they were displeased they could use their magic against you and do you harm.

Secondly, you could never tell when *you* might accidentally come across something that would give you powers of magic or enchantment. You might find the tip of a unicorn's horn, or an old lamp, or a ring, or a walnut shell, or almost anything, and discover that it could be used to tap the power of the invisible beings that control the universe.

Now *that* is exciting!

Suppose you walked into a room, pushed a switch, and the lights went on. So what! Anyone could push a switch. But suppose, on the other hand, you had a little piece of mysterious glass the size of a Ping-Pong ball, and suppose you pulled it out of your pocket and whispered to it the magic words "Fiat lux," and the glass began to glow until it lit the whole room. And suppose that you were the only one who owned such a piece of glass and you were the only one who knew how to make it glow. Wouldn't that be worth a million electric lights?

Or suppose you wanted to know what was going on in Nairobi, Kenya. Wouldn't it be much better to have a crystal ball, and to make magic passes over it, than to just turn on a television set?

Wouldn't it be more fun to fly through the air on the back of a demon than inside an airplane?

Sure it would. Energy and electricity and machinery are all boring. No matter how many scientific marvels we can create, what we really want is magic. We don't want a door to open because we interrupt a beam of light as we walk, or because we step on a hidden pressure device. We want it to open because we say "Open sesame," and we want to be the only one who knows the secret of the phrase.

That is why even in modern times, when we know that magic doesn't work and that energy does, we want to read stories about magic. We still thrill to it and get excited. Even while we read the story by the light of an electric lamp with the air conditioner going, we sigh for the ability to say to a demon, "Light this room and make it cool."

And when the demon says, "Master, I hear and obey,"

how much more exciting that is than to push a switch or two.

So here we have ten stories of witchcraft, warlockry, and magic for you, ten stories in which young people either have or discover unusual powers, and they will please you even in this world of science in which we live.

Ray Bradbury

The April Witch

Did you ever do something and then wonder why?
Maybe this is the answer.

Into the air, over the valleys, under the stars, above
a river, a pond, a road, flew Cecy. Invisible as new
spring winds, fresh as the breath of clover rising from
twilight fields, she flew. She soared in doves as soft
as white ermine, stopped in trees and lived in blos-
soms, showering away in petals when the breeze blew.
She perched in a lime-green frog, cool as mint by a
shining pool. She trotted in a brambly dog and barked
to hear echoes from the sides of distant barns. She
lived in new April grasses, in sweet clear liquids rising
from the musky earth.

It's spring, thought Cecy. I'll be in every living thing
in the world tonight.

Now she inhabited neat crickets on the tar-pool roads,
now prickled in dew on an iron gate. Hers was an

adaptably quick mind flowing unseen upon Illinois winds on this one evening of her life when she was just seventeen.

"I want to be in love," she said.

She had said it at supper. And her parents had widened their eyes and stiffened back in their chairs. "Patience," had been their advice. "Remember, you're remarkable. Our whole family is odd and remarkable. We can't mix or marry with ordinary folk. We'd lose our magical powers if we did. You wouldn't want to lose your ability to 'travel' by magic, would you? Then be careful. Be careful!"

But in her high bedroom, Cecy had touched perfume to her throat and stretched out, trembling and apprehensive, on her four-poster, as a moon the color of milk rose over Illinois country, turning rivers to cream and roads to platinum.

"Yes," she sighed. "I'm one of an odd family. We sleep days and fly nights like black kites on the wind. If we want, we can sleep in moles through the winter, in the warm earth. I can live in anything at all—a pebble, a crocus, or a praying mantis. I can leave my plain, bony body behind and send my mind far out for adventure. Now!"

The wind whipped her away over fields and meadows.

She saw the warm spring lights of cottages and farms glowing with twilight colors.

If I can't be in love, myself, because I'm plain and odd, then I'll be in love through someone else, she thought.

Outside a farmhouse in the spring night a dark-haired girl, no more than nineteen, drew up water from a deep stone well. She was singing.

Cecy fell—a green leaf—into the well. She lay in the tender moss of the well, gazing up through dark coolness. Now she quickened in a fluttering, invisible amoeba. Now in a water droplet! At last, within a cold cup, she felt herself lifted to the girl's warm lips. There was a soft night sound of drinking.

Cecy looked out from the girl's eyes.

She entered into the dark head and gazed from the shining eyes at the hands pulling the rough rope. She listened through the shell ears to this girl's world. She smelled a particular universe through these delicate nostrils, felt this special heart beating, beating. Felt this strange tongue move with singing.

Does she know I'm here? thought Cecy.

The girl gasped. She stared into the night meadows.

"Who's there?"

No answer.

"Only the wind," whispered Cecy.

"Only the wind." The girl laughed at herself, but shivered.

It was a good body, this girl's body. It held bones of finest slender ivory hidden and roundly fleshed. This brain was like a pink tea rose, hung in darkness, and there was cider-wine in this mouth. The lips lay firm on the white, white teeth and the brows arched neatly at the world, and the hair blew soft and fine on her milky neck. The pores knit small and close. The nose tilted at the moon and the cheeks glowed like small fires. The body drifted with feather-balances from one motion to another and seemed always singing to itself. Being in this body, this head, was like basking in a hearth fire, living in the purr of a sleeping cat, stirring in warm creek waters that flowed by night to the sea.

I'll like it here, thought Cecy.

"What?" asked the girl, as if she'd heard a voice.

"What's your name?" asked Cecy carefully.

"Ann Leary." The girl twitched. "Now why should I say *that* out loud?"

"Ann, Ann," whispered Cecy. "Ann, you're going to be in love."

As if to answer this, a great roar sprang from the road, a clatter and a ring of wheels on gravel. A tall man drove up in a rig, holding the reins high with his monstrous arms, his smile glowing across the yard.

"Ann!"

"Is that you, Tom?"

"Who else?" Leaping from the rig, he tied the reins to the fence.

"I'm not speaking to you!" Ann whirled, the bucket in her hands slopping.

"No!" cried Cecy.

Ann froze. She looked at the hills and the first spring stars. She stared at the man named Tom. Cecy made her drop the bucket.

"Look what you've done!"

Tom ran up.

"Look what you *made* me do!"

He wiped her shoes with a kerchief, laughing.

"Get away!" She kicked at his hands, but he laughed again, and gazing down on him from miles away, Cecy saw the turn of his head, the size of his skull, the flare of his nose, the shine of his eye, the girth of his shoulder, and the hard strength of his hands doing this delicate thing with the handkerchief. Peering down from the secret attic of this lovely head, Cecy yanked a hidden copper ventriloquist's wire and the pretty mouth popped wide: "Thank you!"

"Oh, so you *have* manners?" The smell of leather on his hands, the smell of the horse rose from his clothes into the tender nostrils, and Cecy, far, far away over night meadows and flowered fields, stirred as with some dream in her bed.

"Not for you, no!" said Ann.

"Hush, speak gently," said Cecy. She moved Ann's fingers out toward Tom's head. Ann snatched them back.

"I've gone mad!"

"You have." He nodded, smiling but bewildered. "Were you going to touch me then?"

"I don't know. Oh, go away!" Her cheeks glowed with pink charcoals.

"Why don't you run? I'm not stopping you." Tom got up. "Have you changed your mind? Will you go to the dance with me tonight? It's special. Tell you why later."

"No," said Ann.

"Yes!" cried Cecy. "I've never danced. I want to dance. I've never worn a long gown, all rustly. I want that. I want to dance all night. I've never known what it's like to be in a woman, dancing; Father and Mother would never permit it. Dogs, cats, locusts, leaves, everything else in the world at one time or another I've known, but never a woman in the spring, never on a night like this. Oh, please—we *must* go to that dance!"

She spread her thought like the fingers of a hand within a new glove.

"Yes," said Ann Leary, "I'll go. I don't know why, but I'll go to the dance with you tonight, Tom."

"Now inside, quick!" cried Cecy. "You must wash, tell your folks, get your gown ready, out with the iron, into your room!"

"Mother," said Ann, "I've changed my mind!"

*   *   *

The rig was galloping off down the pike, the rooms of the farmhouse jumped to life, water was boiling for a bath, the coal stove was heating an iron to press the gown, the mother was rushing about with a fringe of hairpins in her mouth. "What's come over you, Ann? You don't like Tom!"

"That's true." Ann stopped amidst the great fever.

But it's spring! thought Cecy.

"It's spring," said Ann.

And it's a fine night for dancing, thought Cecy.

". . . for dancing," murmured Ann Leary.

Then she was in the tub and the soap creaming on her white seal shoulders, small nests of soap beneath her arms, and the flesh of her warm breasts moving in her hands and Cecy moving the mouth, making the smile, keeping the actions going. There must be no pause, no hesitation, or the entire pantomime might fall in ruins! Ann Leary must be kept moving, doing, acting, wash here, soap there, now out! Rub with a towel! Now perfume and powder!

"You!" Ann caught herself in the mirror, all whiteness and pinkness like lilies and carnations. "*Who* are you tonight?"

"I'm a girl seventeen." Cecy gazed from her violet eyes. "You can't see me. Do you know I'm here?"

Ann Leary shook her head. "I've rented my body to an April witch, for sure."

"*Close*, very close!" laughed Cecy. "Now, on with your dressing.

The luxury of feeling good clothes move over an ample body! And then the halloo outside.

"Ann, Tom's back!"

"Tell him to wait." Ann sat down suddenly. "Tell him I'm not going to that dance."

"What?" said her mother, in the door.

Cecy snapped back into attention. It had been a fatal relaxing, a fatal moment of leaving Ann's body for only an instant. She had heard the distant sound of horses' hoofs and the rig rambling through moonlit spring country. For a second she thought, I'll go find Tom and sit in his head and see what it's like to be in a man of twenty-two on a night like this. And so she had started quickly across a heather field, but now, like a bird to a cage, flew back and rustled and beat about in Ann Leary's head.

"Ann!"

"Tell him to go away!"

"Ann!" Cecy settled down and spread her thoughts.

But Ann had the bit in her mouth now, "No, no, I hate him!"

I shouldn't have left—even for a moment. Cecy poured her mind into the hands of the young girl, into the heart, into the head, softly, softly. *Stand up*, she thought.

Ann stood.

Put on your coat!
Ann put on her coat.
Now, march!
No! thought Ann Leary.
March!
"Ann," said her mother, "don't keep Tom waiting another minute. You get on out there now and no nonsense. What's come over you?"

"Nothing, Mother. Good night. We'll be home late."

Ann and Cecy ran together into the spring evening.

A room full of softly dancing pigeons ruffling their quiet, trailing feathers, a room full of peacocks, a room full of rainbow eyes and lights. And in the center of it, around, around, around, danced Ann Leary.

"Oh, it *is* a fine evening," said Cecy.

"Oh, it's a fine evening," said Ann.

"You're odd," said Tom.

The music whirled them in dimness, in rivers of song; they floated, they bobbed, they sank down, they arose for air, they gasped, they clutched each other like drowning people and whirled on again, in fan motions, in whispers and sighs, to "Beautiful Ohio."

Cecy hummed. Ann's lips parted and the music came out.

"Yes, I'm odd," said Cecy.

"You're not the same," said Tom.

"No, not tonight."

"You're not the Ann Leary I knew."

"No, not at all, at all," whispered Cecy, miles and miles away. "No, not at all," said the moved lips.

"I've the funniest feeling," said Tom.

"About what?"

"About you." He held her back and danced her and looked into her glowing face, watching for something. "Your eyes," he said, "I can't figure it."

"Do you see *me*?" asked Cecy.

"Part of you's here, Ann, and part of you's not." Tom turned her carefully, his face uneasy.

"Yes."

"Why did you come with me?"

"I didn't want to come," said Ann.

"Why, then?"

"Something made me."

"What?"

"I don't know." Ann's voice was faintly hysterical.

"Now, now, hush, hush," whispered Cecy. "Hush, that's it. Around, around."

They whispered and rustled and rose and fell away in the dark room, with the music moving and turning them.

"But you *did* come to the dance," said Tom.

"I did," said Cecy.

"Here." And he danced her lightly out an open door and walked her quietly away from the hall and the music and the people.

They climbed up and sat together in the rig.

"Ann," he said, taking her hands, trembling. "Ann." But the way he said the name it was as if it wasn't her name. He kept glancing into her pale face, and now her eyes were open again. "I used to love you, you know that," he said.

"I know."

"But you've always been fickle and I didn't want to be hurt."

"It's just as well, we're very young," said Ann.

"No, I mean to say, I'm sorry," said Cecy.

"What *do* you mean?" Tom dropped her hands and stiffened.

The night was warm and the smell of the earth shimmered up all about them where they sat, and the fresh trees breathed one leaf against another in a shaking and rustling.

"I don't know," said Ann.

"Oh, but *I* know," said Cecy. "You're tall and you're the finest-looking man in all the world. This is a good evening; this is an evening I'll alway remember, being with you." She put out the alien cold hand to find his reluctant hand again and bring it back, and warm it and hold it very tight.

"But," said Tom, blinking, "tonight you're here, you're there. One minute one way, the next minute another. I wanted to take you to the dance tonight for old times' sake. I meant nothing by it when I first asked you.

And then, when we were standing at the well, I knew something had changed, really changed, about you. You were different. There was something new and soft, something . . ." He groped for a word. "I don't know, I can't say. The way you looked. Something about your voice. And I know I'm in love with you again."

"No," said Cecy. "With me, with *me*."

"And I'm afraid of being in love with you," he said. "You'll hurt me again."

"I might," said Ann.

No, no, I'd love you with all my heart! thought Cecy. Ann, say it to him, say it for me. Say you'd love him with all your heart.

Ann said nothing.

Tom moved quietly closer and put his hand up to hold her chin. "I'm going away. I've got a job a hundred miles from here. Will you miss me?"

"Yes," said Ann and Cecy.

"May I kiss you good-by, then?"

"Yes," said Cecy before anyone else could speak.

He placed his lips to the strange mouth. He kissed the strange mouth and he was trembling.

Ann sat like a white statue.

"Ann!" said Cecy. "Move your arms, *hold* him!"

She sat like a carved wooden doll in the moonlight.

Again he kissed her lips.

"I do love you," whispered Cecy. "I'm here, it's me

you saw in her eyes, it's me, and I love you if she never will."

He moved away and seemed like a man who had run a long distance. He sat beside her. "I don't know what's happening. For a moment there . . ."

"Yes?" asked Cecy.

"For a moment I thought—" He put his hands to his eyes. "Never mind. Shall I take you home now?"

"Please," said Ann Leary.

He clucked to the horse, snapped the reins tiredly, and drove the rig away. They rode in the rustle and slap and motion of the moonlit rig in the still early, only eleven o'clock spring night, with the shining meadows and sweet fields of clover gliding by.

And Cecy, looking at the fields and meadows, thought, It would be worth it, it would be worth everything to be with him from this night on. And she heard her parents' voices again, faintly, "Be careful! You wouldn't want to lose your magical powers, would you— married to a mere mortal? Be careful. You wouldn't want that."

Yes, yes, thought Cecy, even that I'd give up, here and now, if he would have me. I wouldn't need to roam the spring nights then, I wouldn't need to live in birds and dogs and cats and foxes, I'd need only to be with him. Only him. Only him.

The road passed under, whispering.

"Tom," said Ann at last.

"What?" He stared coldly at the road, the horse, the trees, the sky, the stars.

"If you're ever, in years to come, at any time, in Green Town, Illinois, a few miles from here, will you do me a favor?"

"Perhaps."

"Will you do me the favor of stopping and seeing a friend of mine?" Ann Leary said this haltingly, awkwardly.

"Why?"

"She's a good friend. I've told her of you. I'll give you her address. Just a moment." When the rig stopped at her farm she drew forth a pencil and paper from her small purse and wrote in the moonlight, pressing the paper to her knee. "There it is. Can you read it?"

He glanced at the paper and nodded bewilderedly.

"Cecy Elliott, 12 Willow Street, Green Town, Illinois," he said.

"Will you visit her someday?" asked Ann.

"Someday," he said.

"Promise?"

"What has this to do with us?" he cried savagely. "What do I want with names and papers?" He crumpled the paper into a tight ball and shoved it in his coat.

"Oh, please promise!" begged Cecy.

". . . promise . . ." said Ann.

"All right, all right, now let me be!" he shouted.

I'm tired, thought Cecy. I can't stay. I have to go home. I'm weakening. I've only the power to stay a few hours out like this in the night, traveling, traveling. But before I go . . .

". . . before I go," said Ann.

She kissed Tom on the lips.

"This is *me* kissing you," said Cecy.

Tom held her off and looked at Ann Leary and looked deep, deep inside. He said nothing, but his face began to relax slowly, very slowly, and the lines vanished away, and his mouth softened from its hardness, and he looked deep again into the moonlit face held here before him.

Then he put her off the rig and without so much as a good night was driving swiftly down the road.

Cecy let go.

Ann Leary, crying out, released from prison, it seemed, raced up the moonlit path to her house and slammed the door.

Cecy lingered for only a little while. In the eyes of a cricket she saw the spring night world. In the eyes of a frog she sat for a lonely moment by a pool. In the eyes of a night bird she looked down from a tall, moon-haunted elm and saw the light go out in two farm-houses, one here, one a mile away. She thought of herself and her family, and her strange power, and the fact that no one in the family could ever marry any one of the people in this vast world out here beyond the hills.

"Tom?" Her weakening mind flew in a night bird under the trees and over deep fields of wild mustard. "Have you still got the paper, Tom? Will you come by someday, some year, sometime, to see me? Will you know me then? Will you look in my face and remember then where it was you saw me last and know that you love me as I love you, with all my heart for all time?"

She paused in the cool night air, a million miles from towns and people, above farms and continents and rivers and hills. "Tom?" Softly.

Tom was asleep. It was deep night; his clothes were hung on chairs or folded neatly over the end of the bed. And in one silent, carefully upflung hand upon the white pillow, by his head, was a small piece of paper with writing on it. Slowly, slowly, a fraction of an inch at a time, his fingers closed down upon and held it tightly. And he did not even stir or notice when a blackbird, faintly, wondrously, beat softly for a moment against the clear moon crystals of the window-pane, then, fluttering quietly, stopped and flew away toward the east, over the sleeping earth.

Elizabeth Coatsworth

Witch Girl

The worst thing that can happen to a witch
is to lose her shape.

It was a windy autumn night with clouds blowing across
the stars. Slowly and wearily five travelers moved
down the moorland road.

"Aren't we ever coming to a house, Uncle Philip?"
the little girl asked, trying to stifle a sob.

"Patience, Ann," said the young man.

Her father, at the head of the little procession, was
leading the old white plow-horse on which his wife rode
with the youngest child in her arms. Now, he said
bitterly, "The people at the last inn told us that we
should come to shelter long before this."

Suddenly the little girl came closer to her uncle.

"What was that?" she asked in terror.

"It sounded like a dog howling."

"Or a wolf," her father mumbled.

Philip stooped down and picked up Ann in his arms. "I'll carry you now."

Without halting, they went on, even though the white horse pulled back at the bit and began to sweat and shake.

Suddenly the horse shied. Out of the shadows a figure appeared, walking toward them. Unnoticed, the moon had risen. Now there was light enough for the travelers to see that the newcomer was a young girl in a dark cloak, with dark hair blowing about her face.

She seemed to be out of breath.

"We heard you coming," she said. "My grandmother, my two aunts—we live in a little house, only a mile from here. They are making everything ready for you."

"How kind!" the woman on the horse exclaimed. "And for you to have run to meet us, too! What is your name, my dear?"

The girl hesitated for a moment. "They call me Pretty," she said.

"An unusual name," said the woman, "but it suits you. Do let us go on, John. Poor Whitey is so tired that he shivers all the time."

"Walk with us," said Philip to the girl. "Whitey seems afraid of everything tonight, and you're a stranger, but if you're back here he won't see you."

The girl fell into step beside him, and their eyes met in the moonlight.

"You look tired," said Pretty. "Let me carry the little girl."

"No, I'm all right. Ann's too heavy for you."

The child buried her face in her uncle's shoulder. She seemed afraid.

The little boy in his mother's arms woke with a cry.

"What's the matter, darling?"

"Crows were pecking at my face, Mother."

"That was only a bad dream, dear. Soon we are going to be safe in a house," his mother soothed him. Only she seemed to be entirely unafraid.

Something passed overhead.

"What was that?" Philip asked.

"Only my—" Pretty broke off. "Only a bird."

"It looked very queer and long, almost like a broom."

"The moonlight plays strange tricks. It must have been a night heron with a long bill."

"Yes," said Philip. "It must have been a heron." And they walked on again.

The woman on the white horse began singing a lullaby, her head bent over the drowsing child. The others walked on in silence. Now and then Whitey snorted, as though still afraid.

Over the long moor they saw lighted windows, still far off.

"Now we shall be all right," said the woman. "How good you have been to help us, Pretty."

"I am *not* good," said Pretty, twisting her hands.

"My real name is Pretty Spella, and I am learning to be a witch." Her eyes looked frightened.

"A witch!" everyone exclaimed.

"I'm not much good as a witch," Pretty confessed. "I don't like mixing the brews or making spells to hurt people. But they're raising me to be a witch just the same."

"I'm sure you're a dear, good girl," said the young woman. "If you're in trouble, perhaps we can help you."

"Oh, thank you," said Pretty. She hesitated, and then her words came in a breathless rush.

"I was an orphan and the fat witch called Horrible took me when I was little and has brought me up. She's good to me in her way, but Hag-Chaser hates me because I won't pat Hop-in-the-Fire, her toad. She wants to turn *me* into a toad."

"Mercy me!" said the young mother, and Philip exclaimed suddenly, "We'll take care of you."

"At least forewarned is forearmed," said Ann's father. "Now this young lady had better tell us what we can do to save ourselves, if she knows."

"I know some things about spells, but not everything," said Pretty, who spoke with more confidence since everyone was acting in such a friendly manner.

"In the first place, the house you will see isn't a *real* house. It's made from a square of thistles, bewitched. And the three witches won't look like themselves at all, but like nice country women. Even Grimalkin will have a ribbon around her neck."

Pretty went on telling all she knew with her face very white and earnest in the moonlight, and her eyes very large and bright, and her hair softer than shadows.

"Don't let the children out of your sight for a moment," Pretty warned them. "Whoever eats a single crumb will be in their power. Remember, neither sip nor sup. But if you don't stop at the cottage, they'll send wolves to pursue you, or surround you with fire, or some other awful sorcery. And while you are talking, I will try to find the spell book. It takes different shapes, sometimes large, sometimes small, but it is always oblong. They can't any of them make spells without it. Our only hope lies in destroying the book, and then they will be powerless, and you can escape."

"Yes," said Philip, "and when we leave, Pretty will come with us. And I am going to marry her."

Pretty didn't say yes, and Pretty didn't say no, but in the darkness she flushed as red as a rose. But only Philip noticed.

"We must go on," said the woman on the horse. "They'll be waiting. John, take Ann, and let Philip and Pretty lead Whitey. Everything will be all right."

They were met at the cottage door by three nice-looking old ladies in fresh dresses of sprigged calico. One old lady was rather fat, and one old lady was rather small, and the third old lady was tall as a may-pole. But what of that?

There was a black cat by the hearth asleep on a cushion, and the brooms in the corner behind the door gave a rattle all by themselves when the strangers came in. But what of that? If the fire seemed to talk to itself, and the teakettle whistled like a blackbird, and a big toad hopped hastily off the step as they approached: these things might happen anywhere.

Whitey, who appeared too frightened to whinny, was fastened to the hitching post by the door, and the travelers all went into the low room, bright with candles and warm with fire.

And how the three old ladies welcomed the newcomers! How they helped them off with their cloaks and brought out chairs by the fire for them! How they admired the beautiful children!

"You must be hungry," said the fat old lady.

"Oh, no, thank you. We have eaten," said the young mother, smiling.

The little white-haired lady, no larger than a six-year-old child, climbed onto a stool and got a plate heaped with cookies and tarts from the shelf.

"Now, I know you'll all want some of my sweets," she said. "There are blackberry tarts and blueberry cookies, and the little ones are sprinkled with black walnuts. Take your pick, my bird," she said to the little boy on his mother's lap.

But his mother gently pulled back his hand. "Eating at night gives him bad dreams," she said.

"But you're too old to dream, aren't you, Honeysuckle?" said the little lady, sliding close to Ann, who stood by the fire.

"No, thank you, ma'am," said Ann, looking wistfully at the tarts.

"It's good manners to take one, child!"

"Shall I, Father?" asked Ann.

Her father shook his head. "Eating at night doesn't agree with Ann either."

"Look out!" exclaimed the cat.

The three old ladies immediately stopped what they were doing and looked about the room wildly. There was Pretty in a corner reaching toward a cobweb overhead, on which sat a black, rather oblong-looking spider.

"Let that alone!" shrieked Horrible, waving her arms at Pretty Spella.

"Stop! Stop," shrilled little Scrits.

It was Hag-Chaser who gave a thin, long leap across the room toward the girl, reaching out with her clutching fingers.

Philip stepped in front of Pretty with his staff raised. "Keep back!" he cried.

"Brooms! Brooms! Help!" shrieked the three old ladies together, and instantly three brooms hopped from behind the door and made for Philip and the girl immediately and with great speed. But swifter still, a fourth broom with a red handle came hurrying up from another corner and barred their path.

While the young mother clutched her little boy, and John picked up Ann and carried her out of the way, the battle raged. The old ladies shrieked and the brooms fought, handle clashing against handle. Philip joined the defense of the red broomstick against the others, while the cat yowled and bit his ankle, and the toad came huffing and puffing through a hole in the wainscot.

But Pretty had seized the spider, web and all, and still protected by Philip and the red-handled broom, she gained the hearth and flung the oblong-shaped creature into the flames.

Instantly the fire leaped up into the chimney throat, the brooms fell with a clatter to the floor, and the candles winked low and rose again. Hop-in-the-Fire huffed and puffed back through the hole, Grimalkin returned to her cushion, and the three old ladies began to set their aprons straight, and fluff up the ribbons of their white caps.

"Oh deary me," whimpered little Scrits. "What will become of us now?"

"No one will fear us," mumbled the fat witch called Horrible.

"We'll starve," moaned Hag-Chaser.

The young mother looked troubled. "Can't you just

go on living here?" she said. "It's such a nice cottage."

"But how are we to maintain ourselves, Madam?" said Horrible, crossly.

"Couldn't you weave?"

"I used to weave cloth before I wove spells," said Hag-Chaser unexpectedly, "and Scrits made rag rugs very nicely, long ago when she was young."

"My specialty was linen. That, too, was long ago," added Horrible, "but I still remember."

The three old ladies became quite enthusiastic as they talked.

"It will be a change," said Scrits. "Anything for a change. And we're very near the road. We should get good trade."

"I will send you my cookbook, and you will find it much more fun than a spell book, I know," said the young mother.

"How kind you are, Madam!" exclaimed little Scrits, making an effort to smile. "And now you'd better all be getting on. The village is only a mile beyond us. You go too, Pretty Spella, with your fine young man by your side!"

"Yes, good-bye," said Hag-Chaser. "I always said you'd be our ruin, girl."

"You weren't cut out for a witch, ever," said Horrible kindly. "This new form of life will fit you better, so run along, my dear."

The travelers were glad enough to go. No sip nor

sup had they taken. Whitey, too, was glad to leave the little cottage behind. And Pretty walked with her young man's arm about her, carrying with her the faithful broom with the red handle.

"Oh, not for riding of course," she assured Philip. "I'm done with all that, and the poor thing is only an ordinary broom now, anyway. But we did have some wonderful rides together. It's not wrong for me to remember them, is it?"

"Certainly not," said Philip. "What a good fight it put up tonight! I shall buy a silver hook for it, and it shall hang on our kitchen wall in the place of honor when we are married."

Robert Arthur

The Wonderful Day

Ask and ye shall receive.

I

Danny was crouched on the stairs, listening to the grown-ups talk in the living room below. He wasn't supposed to be there. He was supposed to be in bed, since he was still recovering from the chicken pox.

But it got lonely being in bed all the time, and he hadn't been able to resist slipping out and down in his wool pajamas, to hear Dad and Mom and Sis and Uncle Ben and Aunt Anna talking.

Dad—he was Dr. Norcross, and everybody went to him when they were sick—and the others were playing bridge. Sis, who was in high school, was studying her Latin, not so hard she couldn't take part in the conversation.

They were mostly talking about other people in Locustville, which was such a small town everybody knew everybody else, well enough to talk about them, anyway.

"Locustville!" That was Mom, with a sigh. "I know it's a pretty town, with the river and the trees and the woods around it, and Tom has a good practice here, but the people! If only something would shake some of them out of themselves, and show them how petty and malicious and miserable they are!"

"Like Netty Peters," Dad said, his tone dry. Danny knew Miss Peters. Always hurrying over to some neighbor's to talk about somebody. Whisper-whisper-whisper. Saying nasty things. "She's the source of most of the gossip in this town. If ever there was a woman whose tongue was hinged in the middle and wagged at both ends, it's her."

Uncle Ben laughed.

"Things would be better here," he remarked, "if the money were better distributed. If Jacob Earl didn't own or have a mortgage on half the town, there might be more free thought and tolerance. But nobody in debt to him dares open his mouth."

"Funny thing," Dad put in, "how some men have a knack for making money at other men's expense. Everything Jacob Earl touches seems to mint money for him—money that comes out of someone else's pocket. Like the gravel land he got from John Wiggins. I'd like to see the process reversed sometime."

"But for real miserliness"—that was Aunt Anna, indignant—"Luke Hawks takes all the prizes. I've seen him come into the Fair-Square store to buy things for his children, and the trouble he had letting go his money, you'd have thought it stuck to his fingers!"

"It's a question," Dad said, "which is worse, miserliness or shiftlessness. Miserliness, I suppose, because most shiftless people are at least good-hearted. Like Henry Jones. Henry wishes for more things and does less to get them than any man in Christendom. If wishes were horses, Henry would have the biggest herd this side of the Mississippi."

"Well, there are some nice people in Locustville," Sis broke into the conversation. "I don't care what that old gossip Miss Peters says, or that stuck-up Mrs. Norton either; I think Miss Avery, my English and gym teacher, is swell. She isn't awful pretty, but she's nice.

"There's little silver bells in her voice when she talks, and if that Bill Morrow whose dad owns the implement factory, and who takes time off to coach the football team, wasn't a dope, he'd have fallen for her long ago. She's crazy about him, but too proud to show it, and that silly Betty Norton has made him think he's wonderful by playing up to him all the time."

"If he marries Betty," Aunt Anna said, "the town won't be able to hold Mrs. Norton anymore. She's already so puffed up with being the wife of the bank president and the leader of the town's social life, she'd just swell up a little more and float away like a balloon if she got the Morrow Implement Company for a son-in-law."

Everybody laughed, and the conversation slowly died away.

Mom mentioned how much she disliked the two-faced Minerva Benson who was so nice to people's faces and worked against them behind their backs.

Sis said that Mr. Wiggins, who ran the bookstore, was a nice little man who ought to marry Miss Wilson, the dressmaker, a plain little woman who would be as pretty as a picture if she *looked* the way she *was*.

But he never would, Sis said, because he hadn't any money and would be ashamed to ask a woman to marry him when he couldn't even earn his own living.

Then they went back to bridge. Danny was feeling sort of weak and shaky, so he hurried back to bed before Mom could catch him. He crawled in and pulled the blankets up over him, and then his hand reached under the pillow and pulled out the funny thing he'd found in the old chest where he kept his games and skates and things.

It had been wrapped in a soft piece of leather, and he had found it in a little space behind one of the drawers. There was a name inked on the leather, *Jonas*

Norcross. Dad's grandfather had been named Jonas, so it might have been originally his.

What the thing was, was a little pointed piece of ivory, sharp at the tip and round at the bottom, as if it had been sawed off the very end of an elephant's tusk.

Only there was a fine spiral line in it, like in a snail's shell, that made Danny think maybe it hadn't come from an elephant, but from an animal he had seen in a book once—an animal like a horse, with one long horn over its nose. He couldn't remember the name.

It was all yellow with age, and on the bottom was carved a funny mark, all cross lines, very intricate. Maybe it was Chinese writing. Jonas Norcross had been captain of a clipper ship in the China trade, so it might have come all the way from China.

Lying in bed, Danny held the bit of ivory in his hand. It gave out a warmth to his fingers that was nice. Holding it tight, he thought of a picture in his book about King Arthur's Round Table—a picture of Queen Guinevere of the golden hair. Probably it was a picture like that that Sis had meant Miss Wilson ought to be pretty as.

Grown-ups' talk wasn't always easy to understand, the way they said things that weren't so.

Danny yawned. Gee, though, it would be awful funny— He yawned again, and the weight of drowsiness descending on him closed his eyes. But not before one last thought had floated through his mind.

As it came to him, a queer little breeze seemed to spring up in the room. It fluttered the curtains and rattled the window shade. For just a second Danny felt almost as if somebody was in the room with him. Then it was gone, and smiling at his amusing thought, Danny slept.

II

Henry Jones woke that morning with the smell of frying bacon in his nostrils. He yawned and stretched, comfortably. There was a clock on the bureau on the other side of the room, but it was too much trouble to look at it.

He looked at where the sunshine, coming in the window, touched the carpet. That told him it was just onto nine.

Downstairs pans were rattling. Martha was up and about, long ago. And just about ready to get impatient with him for lingering in bed.

"Ho *huuuum!*" Henry yawned, and pushed down the covers. "I wish I was up an' dressed aw-ready."

As if it were an echo to his yawn, a shrill whickering sound reached him from the direction of his large, untidy backyard. Disregarding it, Henry slid into his trousers and shirt, his socks and shoes, put on a tie, combed his hair casually, and ambled down to the dining room.

"Well!" his wife, Martha, commented tartly, appearing in the doorway with a platter in her hands as he slumped down into his chair. "It's after nine. If you're going to look for work today, you should have been started long ago!"

Henry shook his head dubiously as she set the bacon and eggs in front of him.

"I dunno if I ought to go tramping around today," he muttered. "Don't feel so well. Mmm, that looks good. But I kind of wish we could have sausage oncet in a while."

From the rear yard came another high whinny that went unnoticed.

"Sausage is expensive," Martha told him. "When you get an honest job, maybe we can afford some."

"There's Hawks," Henry remarked, with interest, peering out the front window as a lean, long-faced man strode past his house, with a pleasant but shabbily dressed little woman trotting meekly at his side. "Guess Millie has talked him into laying out some money for new things for the kids at last. It's only about once a year she gets him to loosen up."

"And then you'd think, to look at him, he was dying," his wife commented, "just because he's buying a couple of pairs of two-dollar shoes for two as nice youngsters as ever lived. He begrudges them every mouthful they eat, almost."

"Still," Henry said, wagging his head wisely, "I wish I had the money he has stacked away."

From the rear yard came a sound of galloping hooves. Martha was too intent on scolding Henry to notice it.

"Wish, wish, wish!" she stormed. "But never work, work, work! Oh, Henry, you're the most exasperating man alive!"

"Martha, I'm not worthy of you," Henry sighed. "I wish you had a better husband. I mean it."

This time the whinnying behind the house was a concerted squeal from many throats, too loud to go unnoticed. Henry's buxom wife started, looked puzzled, and hurried out to the kitchen. A moment later her screech reached Henry's ears.

"Henry! The backyard's full of horses! Plunging and kicking all over the place!"

The news was startling enough to overcome Henry's early-morning lethargy. He joined his wife at the kitchen window and stared with popping eyes at the big rear yard.

It was full—anyway, it seemed full—of animals. Martha had called them horses. They weren't exactly horses. But they weren't ponies either. They were too small to be the one and too big to be the other. And they were covered with longish hair, had wild flowing manes, and looked strong and savage enough to lick their weight in tigers.

"Well, I'll be deuced!" Henry exclaimed, his round countenance vastly perplexed. "I wish I knew where those critters came from."

"Henry!" Martha wailed, clutching his arm. "Now there's five!"

There had been four of them, trotting about the yard, nosing at the wreck of the car Henry had once driven, thumping with their hooves the board fence that penned them in. But now there were, indeed, five.

"G-gosh!" Henry gulped, his Adam's apple working up and down. "We must have counted wrong. Now, how do you suppose they got in there?"

"But what kind of horses are they, Henry?" Martha asked, holding to his arm still, as if for protection, in a way she hadn't for years. "And whom do you suppose they belong to?"

Henry put an arm around Martha's plump waist and applied a reassuring pressure.

"I wish I knew, Martha," he muttered. "I wish I knew."

"Henry!" There was real fright in his wife's voice. "Now there's six!"

"Seven," Henry corrected weakly. "The other two just—just sort of appeared."

Together they gazed at the seven shaggy ponies that were trotting restlessly about the yard, nosing at the fence as if seeking escape from the limited space.

No more appeared; and seeing the number remain stable, Henry and Martha gained more self-possession.

"Henry," his wife said with severity, as if somehow blaming him, "there's something queer happening. Nobody ever saw horses like those in Indiana before."

"Maybe they belong to a circus," Henry suggested, staring in fascination at the seven uncouth beasts.

"Maybe they belong to us!"

"Us?" Henry's jaw dropped. "How could they belong to us?"

"Henry," his wife told him, "you've got to go out and see if they're branded. I remember reading anybody can claim a wild horse if it hasn't been branded. And those are wild horses if I ever saw any."

Of course, Martha never *had* seen any wild horses, but her words sounded logical. Her husband, however, made no motion toward the back door.

"Listen," he said, "Martha, you stay here and watch. Don't let anybody into the yard. I'm going to get Jake Harrison, at the stable. He used to be a horse trader. He'll know what those things are and if they belong to us, if anybody does."

"All right, Henry," his wife agreed—the first time he could remember her agreeing with him in, anyway, two years—"but hurry. Please do hurry."

"I will!" Henry vowed; and without even snatching up his hat, he shot away.

Jake Harrison, the livery stable owner, came back with him unwillingly, half dragged in Henry's excitement. But when he stood in the kitchen and stared out at the yard full of horses, his incredulity vanished.

"Good Lord!" he gasped. "Henry, where'd you get 'em?"

"Never mind that," Henry told him. "Just tell me, what *are* they?"

"Mongolian ponies," the lanky horse dealer informed him. "The exact kind of ponies old Ghengis Khan's men rode on when they conquered most of the known world. I've seen pictures of them in books. Imagine it! Mongolian ponies here in Locustville!"

"Well," Martha asked, with withering scorn, "aren't you going out to see if they're branded? Or are you two men afraid of a lot of little ponies?"

"I guess they won't hurt us," the stable owner decided, "if we're careful. Come on, Henry, let's see if I'm still any good at lassoing. Mis' Jones, can I use this hank of clothesline?"

Henry opened the kitchen door and followed Jake Harrison out into the yard. At their advent the seven ponies—he was glad to see the number hadn't changed in his absence—stopped their restless trotting and lifted their heads to stare at the men.

Jake made a noose out of the clothesline and began to circle it above his head. The ponies snorted and reared suspiciously. Picking the smallest one, the tall man let the noose go, and it settled over the creature's thick neck.

The pony's nostrils flared. It reared and beat the air with its unshod front hooves as the other six broke and scampered to the opposite end of the yard.

Jake Harrison drew the loop tight and approached the pony, making soothing sounds. It quieted and, as the two men came close, let Jake put his hands on it.

"Yes, sir," the stable owner exclaimed, "a real honest-to-Homer Mongolian pony. That long hair is to keep the cold out, up in the mountains of Tibet. Now let's see if there's any brand. None on its hide. Let's see its hoof."

The pony let him lift its left forefoot without protest, and Henry, bending close, let out a whoop.

"Look, Jake!" he yelled. "It's branded! With my name! These critters are mine!"

Together they stared. Cut into the hard horn, in neat letters, was HENRY JONES.

Jake straightened.

"Yours, all right," he agreed. "Now, Henry, stop making a mystery and tell me where these animals came from."

Henry's jubilance faded. He shook his head.

"Honest, Jake, I don't know. I wish I did. . . . *Look out!*"

The tall man leaped back. Between them an eighth

pony had appeared, so close that its flanks brushed against them.

"W-where—" Jake stuttered, backing away toward the door in the fence and fumbling for the catch. "Where—"

"That's what I don't know!" Henry joined him. "That's what I wish— No, I don't either! I don't wish anything at all!"

The phantom pony that had appeared directly before them, wispy and tenuous as darkish smoke, promptly vanished.

Henry mopped his face.

"Did you see what I saw?" he asked; and Jake, swallowing hard, nodded.

"You st-started to wish for something, and it st-started to appear," he gobbled, and thrust open the door in the board fence. "Let's get out o' here."

"When I started to wish— Oh, jiminy crickets!" Henry groaned. "That's how the others happened. When I wished. Do you suppose— Do you—"

Pale-faced, they stared at each other. Slowly the stableman nodded.

"Lord!" the ashen Henry whispered. "I never believed such a thing could happen. I wish now I'd never—"

This time the words weren't fully out of his mouth before the ninth pony struck the earth with a sudden plop directly before them.

It was too much. Henry broke and ran, and Jake followed at his heels. The pony, interestedly, chased them. Its brothers, not to be left behind, streamed through the opening in the fence, whickering gleefully.

When Henry and Jake brought up, around the corner of the house, they were just in time to look back and see the last of the beasts trotting out into Main Street. Nine wicked whinnies cut through the morning quiet. Nine sets of small hooves pounded.

"They're stampeding!" Henry shrilled. "Jake, we got to round 'em up before they do lots of damage. Oh, Jehoshaphat, I wish this hadn't ever happened!"

Neighing raucously, the tenth pony kicked up its heels, throwing dirt in their faces, and set off at a gallop after the others.

III

About the time Henry Jones was running for Jake Harrison, Luke Hawks was fingering a boy's woolen suit with lean, predatory digits.

"This be the cheapest?" he asked, and being assured that it was—all the clerks in Locustville knew better than to show him anything but the least expensive— nodded.

"I'll take it," he said, and grudgingly reached for his hip pocket.

"Don't you think the material is kind of thin, Luke?" little Emily Hawks asked, a note of pleading in her voice. "Last winter Billy had colds all the time, and Ned—"

The man did not bother to answer. With the well-filled wallet in his left hand, he inserted thumb and forefinger and brought out a twenty-dollar bill.

"Here," he said. "And I've got thirteen dollars forty cents coming."

Taking the bill and starting to turn away, the clerk turned abruptly back. Luke Hawks had snatched the money from his hand.

"Is anything—" he began and stopped. Testily the man was still holding out the note.

"Take it," he snapped. "Don't make me stand here waiting."

"Yes, sir." The clerk apologized, and took a firmer hold. But he could not take the bill from Luke Hawks. He pulled. Hawks' hand jerked forward. Scowling, the lean man drew his hand back. The money came with it.

"What's the matter, Luke?" Emily Hawks asked. Her husband favored her with a frown.

"Some glue on it, or something," he muttered. "It stuck to my fingers. I'll get another bill out, young man."

He put the twenty back into the wallet—where it went easily enough—and drew out two tens. But neither would these leave his hand.

Luke Hawks was beginning to go a little pale. He transferred the notes to his left hand. But though his left hand could take them from his right, the clerk could take them from neither. Whenever he tugged at it, the money simply would not come loose. It stuck as close to Luke Hawks' fingers as if it were part of his skin.

A red flush crept into the man's cheeks. He could not meet his wife's gaze.

"I—I dunno—" he muttered. "I'll lay it down. You pick it up."

Carefully he laid a ten-dollar bill on the counter, spread his fingers wide, and lifted his hand. To his horror and fright, the bit of green paper came with it, adhering firmly to his fingertips.

"Luke Hawks," his wife said sturdily, "it's a judgment on you. The good Lord has put a curse on your money."

"Hush!" Hawks warned. "Netty Peters has come in the store and is looking. She'll hear you and go gabbing nonsense all—"

"It is not nonsense!" his wife stated. "It's truth. Your money will not leave your fingers."

Luke Hawks went deathly pale again. With a strangled curse, he snatched out all the money in his wallet and tried to throw it down on the counter. To his intense relief, one folded green slip fluttered down, though the rest remained in his hand.

"There!" he gasped. "It ain't so! Boy, how much is that?"

The clerk reached for the paper.

"It—it's a cigar coupon, sir," he reported, his face wooden.

Luke Hawks wilted then. He thrust all his money into the ancient pigskin wallet and, being careful his fingers touched only the leather, held it out to his wife.

"Here!" he directed. "You pay him, Emily."

Emily Hawks folded her arms and looked straight into his frightened eyes.

"Luke Hawks," she said, in a firm, clear voice that carried through the entire store, "for eight years my life has been made a misery by your mean, grasping ways. Now you can't spend any of your money. You'll starve to death before you can even spend a nickel for bread.

"And I've a good mind to let you. If I don't buy anything for you, you can be sure no one will give it to you. The people of this town would laugh themselves sick seeing you with your hands full of money, begging for a bite to eat. They wouldn't give it to you either."

Luke Hawks knew they wouldn't. He stared down at his wife, who had never before dared act like this.

"No," he protested. "Emily, don't say that. Here,

you take the money. Spend it as you want. Get the things we need. I'll leave it all to you. You—you can even get the next most expensive clothes for the boys."

"You mean you want me to handle the money from now on?" Emily Hawks demanded, and her husband nodded.

"Yes, Emily," he gasped. "Take it. Please take it."

His wife took the wallet—which left Luke Hawks' hands readily enough—and counted the money in it.

"Five hundred dollars," she said aloud, thoughtfully. "Luke, hadn't you better give me a check for what you've got in the bank? If I'm to do all the buying, the money'll have to be in my hands."

"A check!" Luke exclaimed. "That's it! I don't need money. I'll pay by check."

"Try it," Emily invited. "That's the same as cash, isn't it?"

Luke tried it. The check would not leave his fingers either. It only tore to pieces when the clerk tugged at it.

After that, he capitulated. He took out his book and signed a blank check, which Emily was able to take. She then filled it in for herself for the entire balance in the bank—twenty thousand dollars, Luke Hawks admitted with strangled reluctance.

After that she tucked the check into the bosom of her dress.

"Now, Luke," she suggested, "you might as well go on home. I'll go to the bank and deposit this to my account. Then I'll do the rest of the shopping. I won't need you."

"But how'll you get the things home?" her husband asked weakly.

Emily Hawks was already almost to the door—out which Netty Peters had just dashed to spread the news through the town. But she paused long enough to turn and smile brightly at her pale and perspiring husband.

"I'll have the man at the garage drive me out with them," she answered. "In the car I'm going to buy after I leave the bank, Luke."

IV

Miss Wilson looked up from her sewing at the sound of galloping hooves in the street outside her tiny shop.

She was just in time to see a small swift figure race by. Then, before she could wonder what it was, she caught sight of herself in the big mirror customers used when trying on the dresses she made.

Her whole name was Alice Wilson. But it was years since anyone had called her by her first name. She was thirty-three, as small and plain as a church mouse—

But she wasn't! Miss Wilson stared open-mouthed at her reflection. She—she wasn't mouselike any longer. She was—yes, really—almost pretty!

A length of dress goods forgotten in one hand, a needle suspended in midair in the other, Alice Wilson stared at the woman in the glass. A small woman, with a smiling, pink and white face, over which a stray lock of golden hair had fallen from the piled-up mass of curls on the top of her head—curls that gave out a soft and shining light.

The woman in the mirror had soft, warm red lips and blue eyes of sky-azure clearness and depth. Alice Wilson stared, and smiled in sheer delight. The image smiled back.

Wonderingly, Alice touched her face with her fingers. What had happened? What kind of a trick were her eyes playing on her? How—

The clatter of hurrying footsteps made her jump. Netty Peters, her sharp face alight with excitement, her head thrust forward on her skinny neck like a running chicken's, ran in. Miss Wilson's dressmaking shop, the closest place to the Fair-Square store, was her first stop on her tour to spread the news of Luke Hawks' curse.

"Miss Wilson," she gobbled breathlessly, "what do you think—"

"She thinks you've come to spread some scandal or

other, that's what she thinks," a shrill, file-like voice interrupted.

The voice seemed to come from her own mouth. Netty Peters glared.

"Miss Wilson," she snapped, "if you think ventriloquism is funny when I'm trying to tell you—*just like you're going to tell everybody else!"* the second voice broke in, and Netty Peters felt faint. The words *had* come from her own mouth!

She put her hands to her throat; and because her mind was blank with fright, her tongue went busily ahead with what she had planned to say.

"I saw Luke Hawks—*just like you see everything"*—that was the shrill, second voice, alternating with her own normal one—"in the Fair-Square store and they—*were minding their own business, something you might do*—and they were buying clothes for their poor starved children whom they treat so shamefully—*trust you to get that in!*—when Mr. Hawks tried to pay the clerk—*and you were watching to see how much they spent*—the money wouldn't leave his fingers—*did you ever think how many people would be happy if sometimes the words wouldn't leave your throat?"*

The town gossip ceased. Her words had become all jumbled together, making no sense, like two voices trying to shout each other down. There was a strange

fluttering in her throat. As if she were talking with
two tongues at the same time. . . .

Miss Wilson was staring at her strangely, and Netty
Peters saw for the first time the odd radiance in Miss
Wilson's hair, the new sweetness in her features.

Incoherent words gurgled in the older woman's throat.
Terror glazed her eyes. She turned, and with a queer
sobbing wail, fled.

Alice Wilson was still looking after her in bewilderment when another figure momentarily darkened the
doorway. It was Mr. Wiggins, who owned the un-
profitable bookstore on the other side of her dressmaking establishment.

Ordinarily Mr. Wiggins was a shy, pale-faced man,
his thirty-eight years showing in the stoop of his shoulders, his eyes squinting behind thick glasses. He often
smiled, but it was the small, hopeful smile of a man
who didn't dare not to smile for fear he might lose
heart altogether.

But today, this day of strange happenings, Mr. Wiggins was standing erect. His hair was rumpled, his
glasses were awry, and his eyes blazed with excitement.

"Miss Wilson!" he cried. "The most amazing thing
has happened! I had to tell somebody. I hope you don't
mind my bursting in to tell you."

Alice Wilson stared at him, and instantly forgot about
the strange thing that had happened to her.

"Oh, *no!*" she answered. "Of course I don't. I—I'm glad!"

Outside there were more sounds of galloping hooves, shrill squeals, and men's voices shouting.

"There seems to be a herd of wild ponies loose in the town," Mr. Wiggins told Miss Wilson. "One almost knocked me down, racing along the sidewalk as I was coming here. Miss Wilson, you'll never believe it, what I was going to tell you. You'll have to see for yourself. Then you won't think I'm mad."

"Oh, I'd never think that!" Miss Wilson assured him.

Scarcely hearing her, Mr. Wiggins seized her by the hand and almost dragged her to the door. A flush of warm pleasure rose into Miss Wilson's cheeks at the touch of his hand.

A little breathless, she ran beside him, out the shop door, down a dozen yards, and into the gloom of his tiny, unpatronized bookstore.

On the way, she barely had a glimpse of three or four shaggy ponies snorting and wheeling farther up the street, with Henry Jones and Jake Harrison, assisted by a crowd of laughing men and boys, trying to catch them.

Then Mr. Wiggins, trembling with excitement, was pushing her down into an old overstuffed chair.

"Miss Wilson," he said tensely, "I was sitting right here when in came Jacob Earl, not fifteen minutes ago. You know how he walks—big and pompous, as if he owned the earth. I knew what he wanted. He wanted the thousand dollars I owe him, that I borrowed to buy my stock of books with. And I—I didn't have it. None of it.

"You remember when my aunt died last year, she left me that property down by the river that I sold to Jacob Earl for five hundred dollars? He pretended he was just doing me a favor buying it, to help me get started in business.

"But then high-grade gravel was discovered on the land, and now it's worth at least fifteen thousand dollars. I learned Earl knew about the gravel all the time. But in spite of that, he wanted the thousand he loaned me."

"Yes, oh, yes!" Miss Wilson exclaimed. "He would. But what did you *do*, Mr. Wiggins?"

Mr. Wiggins combed back his disheveled hair with his fingers.

"I told him I didn't have it. And he took off his glove—his right glove—and told me if I didn't have it by tomorrow, he'd have to attach all my books and fixtures. And then he put his hand down on top of my little brass Chinese luck piece. And guess what happened!"

"Oh, I couldn't!" Miss Wilson whispered. "I never could!"

"Look!" Mr. Wiggins' voice trembled. He snatched

up a large dust cloth that hid something on the counter just in front of Miss Wilson's eyes. Underneath the cloth was a squat little Chinese god, about a foot high, sitting with knees crossed and holding a bowl in his lap.

On his brass countenance was a sly smile, and his mouth was open in a round O of great amusement.

And as Miss Wilson stared at him, a small gold coin popped out of the little god's mouth and landed with a musical clink in the bowl in his lap!

Alice Wilson gasped. "Oh, John!" she cried, using Mr. Wiggins' Christian name for the first time in her life. "Is it—is it money?"

"Chinese money," Mr. Wiggins told her. "And the bowl is full of it. A gold coin comes out of his mouth every second. The first one came out right after Mr. Earl put his hand on the god's head. Look!"

He scooped up the contents of the bowl and held them out, let them rain into Miss Wilson's lap. Incredulously she picked one up.

It was a coin as large perhaps as an American nickel. In the center was punched a square hole. All around the edges were queer Oriental ideographs. And the piece of money was as fresh and new and shiny as if it had just come from the mint.

"Is it real gold?" she asked tremulously.

"Twenty carats pure at least!" John Wiggins assured

her. "Even if it is Chinese money, the coins must be worth five dollars apiece just for the metal. And look—the bowl is half full again."

They stared wide-eyed and breathless at the little grinning god. Every second, as regularly as clockwork, another gold coin popped out of his open mouth.

"It's as if—as if he were coining them!" John Wiggins whispered.

"Oh, it's wonderful!" Alice Wilson told him, with rapture. "John, I'm so glad! For your sake. Now you can pay off Earl."

"In his own coin!" the man chortled. "Because he started it happening, you know, so you could call it his own coin. Perhaps he pressed a secret spring or something that released them from where they were hidden inside the god. I don't know.

"But the funny thing is, he couldn't pick them up! He tried to pretend he had just dropped the first couple, but they rolled out of the bowl and right across the floor when he reached for them. And then he began to get frightened. He grabbed up his hat and his gloves and ran out."

Then John Wiggins paused. He was looking down at Alice Wilson, and for the first time he really saw the change that had occurred in her.

"Why—why—" he said, "do you know, your hair is the same color as the coins?"

"Oh, it isn't!" Miss Wilson protested, blushing scar-

let at the first compliment a man had paid her in ten
years.

"It is," he insisted. "And you—you're lovely, Alice.
I never realized before how lovely. You're as pretty
as—as pretty as a picture!"

He looked down into her eyes, and without taking
his gaze away, reached down and took her hands in
his. He drew her up out of the chair, and still crim-
soning with pleasure, Alice Wilson stood and faced
him.

"Alice," John Wiggins said, "Alice, I've known you
for a long time, and I've been blind. I guess worry
blinded me. Or I'd have seen long ago how beautiful
you are and known what I've just realized. I know I'm
not much of a success as a man but—but, Alice, would
you be my wife?"

Alice Wilson gave a little sigh and rested her face
against his shoulder so that he might not see the tears
in her eyes. Happiness had mostly eluded her until
now, but this moment more than made up for all the
years that were past.

John Wiggins put his arms about her, and behind
them the little god grinned and went busily on with
his minting. . . .

Jacob Earl stamped into his library in his home and
locked the door behind him, with fingers that shook a
little.

Throwing his hat and stick down, with his gloves,

onto a chair, he groped for a cigar in his desk and lit it, by sheer force of will striving to quell the inward agitation that was shaking him.

But—well, any man might feel shaken if he had put his hand down on a cold brass paperweight and had felt the thing twist in his grip as if alive, had felt a shock in his fingers like a sudden discharge of electricity, and then had seen the thing start to spout gold money.

Money—and Jacob Earl gazed down at his soft, plump white hands almost with fright—which had *life* in it. Because when he had tried to pick it up, it had eluded him. It had *dodged.*

Angrily he flung away his barely smoked cigar. Hallucinations! He'd been having a dizzy spell, or—or something. Or Wiggins had fixed up a trick to play on him. That was it, a trick!

The nerve of the man, giving him such a start! When he had finished with the little rabbit, he—he—

Jacob Earl did not quite formulate what he would do. But the mere thought of threatening somebody made him feel better. He'd decide later what retaliation he would make.

Right now, he'd get to work. He'd inventory his strong box. Nothing like handling hard, tangible possessions, like stocks and bonds and gold, to restore a man's nerves when he felt shaky.

He spun the combination of his safe, swung open the heavy outer door, unlocked the inner door, and slid out first a weighty steel cash box locked by a massive padlock.

Weighty, because it held the one thing a man couldn't have too much of—gold. Pure gold ingots, worth five hundred dollars each. Fifteen thousand dollars' worth of them.

He'd had them since long before the government called in gold. And he was going to keep them, government or no. If he ever had to sell them, he'd claim they'd been forgotten, and found again by accident.

Jacob Earl flung open the lid of his gold cache. And his overly ruddy face turned a sudden pallid gray. Two of the ingots in the top layer were missing!

But no one could get into his safe. No one but himself. It wasn't possible that a thief—

Then the gray of his face turned to ashen white. He stared, his breath caught in his throat. As he stared, a third ingot had vanished. Evaporated. Into thin air. As if an unseen hand had closed over it and snatched it away.

But it wasn't possible! Such a thing couldn't happen.

And then the fourth ingot vanished. Transfixed by rage and fright, he put his hands down on the remaining yellow bars and pressed with all his might.

But presently the fifth of his precious chunks of metal

slipped away from beneath his very fingers into nothingness. One instant it was there, and he could feel it. Then—gone!

With a hoarse cry, Jacob Earl dropped the cash box. He stumbled across the room to his telephone, got a number.

"Doctor?" he gasped. "Doctor Norcross? This is Jacob Earl. I—I—"

Then he bethought himself. This couldn't happen. This was madness. If he told anyone—

"Never mind, Doctor!" he blurted. "Sorry to have troubled you. It's all right."

He hung up. And sat there, all the rest of the day, sweat beading his brow, watching the shiny yellow oblongs that had fallen on the floor vanish one by one.

In another part of town, another hand crept toward the telephone—and drew back. Minerva Benson's hand. Minerva Benson had discovered her deformity almost the instant she had arisen, late that morning. The stiff, lifeless face affixed to the back of her head now. Thin, vicious, twisted, the features of a harpy.

With trembling fingers she touched it again, in a wild hope that it might have vanished. Then she huddled closer on the end of the sofa in the darkened room, whose door was locked, blinds drawn.

She couldn't telephone. Because no one must see her like this. No one. Not even a doctor. . . .

And in her tiny, spinsterish home Netty Peters also crouched, and also feared to telephone.

Feared, lest that strange, dreadful second voice begin to clack and rattle in her throat when she tried to talk, tried to ask Doctor Norcross to come.

Crouched, and felt her throat with fingers like frantic claws. And was sure she could detect something moving in her throat like a thing alive.

V

Mrs. Edward Norton moved along the tree-shaded streets toward the downtown section of Locustville with all the self-conscious pride of a frigate entering a harbor under full sail.

She was a full-bodied woman—well built, she phrased it—and expensively dressed. Certainly the best-dressed woman in town, as befitted her position as leader of Locustville's social life and the most influential woman in town.

And today she was going to use her influence. She

was going to have Janice Avery discharged as teacher in the high school.

Distinctly she had seen the young woman *smoking* in her room, the previous evening, as she happened to be driving by. A woman who should be an example to the children she taught actually—

Mrs. Norton sailed along, indignation high in her. She had called first at Minerva Benson's home. Minerva was a member of the school board. But Minerva had said she was sick, and refused to see her.

Then she had tried Jacob Earl, the second member of the board. And he had been ill too.

It was odd.

Now she was going directly to the office of Doctor Norcross. He was head of the school board. Not the kind of man she approved of for the position, of course—

Mrs. Norton paused. For the past few moments she had been experiencing a strange sensation of puffiness, of lightness. Was she ill too? Could she be feeling light-headed or dizzy?

But no, she was perfectly normal. Just a moment's upset perhaps, from walking too fast.

She continued onward. What had she been thinking? Oh, yes, Doctor Norcross. An able physician, perhaps, but his wife was really quite—well, quite a dowdy. . . .

Mrs. Norton paused again. A gentle breeze was blowing down the street and she—she was being swayed from side to side by it. Actually, it was almost pushing her off balance!

She took hold of a convenient lamppost. That stopped her from swaying. But—

She stared transfixed at her fingers. They were swollen and puffy.

Her rings were cutting into them painfully. Could she have some awful—

Then she became aware of a strained, uncomfortable feeling all over her person. A feeling of being confined, intolerably pent up in her clothing.

With her free hand she began to pat herself, at first with puzzlement, then with terror. Her clothing was as tight on her as the skin of a sausage. It had shrunk! It was cutting off her circulation!

No, it hadn't. That wasn't true. She was growing! Puffing up! Filling out her clothes like a slowly expanding balloon.

Her corset was confining her diaphragm, making it impossible to breathe. She couldn't get air into her lungs.

She had some awful disease. That was what came of living in a dreadful, dirty place like Locustville, among backward, ignorant people who carried germs and—

At that instant the laces of Mrs. Norton's corsets gave way. She could actually feel herself swell, bloat, puff out. Her arms were queer and hard to handle. The seams of her dress were giving way.

The playful breeze pushed her, and she swayed back and forth like a midnight drunk staggering homeward.

Her fingers slipped from the lamppost.

And she began to rise slowly, ponderously into the air, like a runaway balloon.

Mrs. Edward Norton screamed. Piercingly. But her voice seemed lost, a thin wail that carried hardly twenty yards. This was unthinkable. This was impossible!

But it was happening.

Now she was a dozen feet above the sidewalk. Now twenty. And at that level she paused, spinning slowly around and around, her arms flopping like a frightened chicken's wings, her mouth opening and closing like a feeding goldfish's, but no sounds coming forth.

If anyone should see her now! Oh, if anyone should see her!

But no one did. The street was quite deserted. The houses were few, and set well back from the street. And the excitement downtown, the herd of strange ponies that all day had been kicking up their heels, as Henry Jones and his volunteer assistants tried to pen them up, had drawn every unoccupied soul in Locustville.

Mrs. Norton, pushed along by the gentle breeze, began to drift slowly northward toward the town limits.

Tree branches scraped her and ripped her stockings as she clutched unavailingly at them. A crow, attracted by the strange spectacle, circled around her several times, emitted a raucous squawk that might have been amusement, and flew off.

A stray dog, scratching fleas in the sunshine, saw her pass overhead and followed along underneath for a moment, barking furiously.

Mrs. Norton crimsoned with shame and mortification. Oh, if anyone saw her!

But if no one saw her, no one could help her. She did not know whether to pray for someone to come along or not. She was unhurt. Perhaps nothing worse was going to happen.

But to be sailing placidly through the air, twenty feet above the street, puffed up like a balloon!

The breeze had brought her out to a district marked for subdivision, but still vacant. Fruit trees grew upon the land. The playful wind, shifting its quarter, altered her course. In a moment she was drifting past the upper branches of gnarled old apple trees, quite hidden from the street.

Her clothes were torn, her legs and arms scratched; her hair was straggling down her back. And her indignation and fear of being seen began to give way to a sensation of awful helplessness. She, the most important woman in Locustville, to be blowing around among a lot of old fruit trees for crows to caw at and dogs to bark at and—

Mrs. Norton gasped. She had just risen another three feet.

With that she began to weep.

The tears streamed down her face. All at once she felt humble and helpless and without a thought for her dignity or her position. She just wanted to get down.

She just wanted to go home and have Edward pat her shoulder and say "There, there," as he used to— a long time ago—while she had a good cry on his shoulder.

She was a bad woman, and being punished for it. She had been puffed up with pride, and this was what came of it. In the future, if ever she got down safely, she'd know better.

As if influenced by the remorseful thoughts, she began to descend slowly. Before she was aware of it, she had settled into the upper branches of a cherry tree, scaring away a flock of indignant robins.

And there she caught.

She had quite a lot of time in which to reflect before she saw Janice Avery swinging past along a short cut from the school to her home, and called to her.

Janice Avery got her down. With the aid of Bill Morrow, who was the first person she could find when she ran back to the school to get aid.

Bill was just getting into his car to drive out to the football field, where he was putting the school team through spring practice, when she ran up; and at first he did not seem to understand what she was saying.

As a matter of fact, he didn't. He was just hearing her voice—a voice that was cool and sweet and lovely, like music against a background of distant silver bells.

Then, when he got it, he sprang into action.

"Good Lord!" he exclaimed. "Mrs. Norton stuck up a tree picking cherries? I can't believe it."

But he got a ladder from the school and brought it, gulping at the sight of the stout, tearful woman caught in the crotch of the cherry tree.

A few moments later they had her down. Mrs. Norton made no effort to explain beyond the simple statement she had first made to Janice.

"I was picking cherries and I just got stuck."

Wild as it was, it was better than the truth.

Bill Morrow brought his car as close as he could and Janice hurried her out to it, torn, scratched, bedraggled, red-eyed. They got her in without anyone seeing and drove her home.

Mrs. Norton sobbed out a choked thanks and fled into the house, to weep on the shoulders of her surprised husband.

Bill Morrow mopped his forehead and looked at Janice Avery. She wasn't pretty, but—well, there was something in her face. Something swell. And her voice. A man could hear a voice like that all his life and not grow tired of it.

"Lord!" he exclaimed, as he slid behind the wheel of his car. "And Betty Norton is going to look just like that someday. Whew! Do you know, I'm a fool. I actually once thought of— But never mind. Where can I take you?"

He grinned at her, and Janice Avery smiled back, little happy lines springing into life around the corners of her lips and her eyes.

"Well," she began, as the wide-shouldered young man kicked the motor into life, "you have to get to practice—"

"Practice is out!" Bill Morrow told her with great firmness, and let in the clutch. "We're going someplace and talk!"

She sat back, content.

VI

The sun was setting redly as Dr. Norcross closed his office and swung off homeward with a lithe step.

It had been a strange day. Very strange. Wild ponies had been running through the town since morning, madly chased by the usually somnolent Henry Jones.

From his window he had seen into the bookstore across the street and distinctly perceived John Wiggins and Alice Wilson embracing.

Then there had been that abortive phone call from an obviously agitated Jacob Earl. And he had positively seen Mrs. Luke Hawks going past in a brand-new car, with a young man at the wheel who seemed to be teaching her to drive. Whew!

There would be a lot to tell his wife tonight.

His reflections were cut short as he strode past Henry Jones's backyard, which lay on his homeward short-cut route.

A crowd of townsfolk were gathered about the door in the fence around the yard, and Dr. Norcross could observe others in the house, peering out the windows.

Henry and Jake Harrison, mopping their faces with fatigue, stood outside peering into the yard through the cautiously opened doorway. And over the fence itself, he was able to see the tossing heads of many ponies, while their squeals cut the evening air.

"Well, Henry"—that was Martha, who came around the corner of the house and pushed through the crowd about her husband—"you've rounded up all the horses all right. But how're you going to pay for the damage they did today? Now you'll have to go to work, in spite of yourself. Even if they aren't good for anything else they've accomplished *that*!"

There was an excitement on Henry's face Dr. Norcross had never seen there before.

"Sure, Martha, sure," he agreed. "I know I'll have to pay off the damage. But Jake and me, we've got plans for these hooved jackrabbits. Know what we're going to do?"

He turned, so all of the gathered crowd could hear his announcement.

"Jake and me, we're going to use that land of Jake's south of town to breed polo ponies!" he declared. "Yes, sir, we're going to cross these streaks of lightning with real polo ponies. We're gonna get a new breed with the speed of a whippet, the endurance of a mule, and the intelligence of a human.

"Anybody who seen these creatures skedaddle around town today knows that when we get a polo pony with their blood in it developed, it'll be something! Yes, sir, something! I wish—

"No I don't! I don't wish anything! Not a single, solitary thing! I'm not gonna wish for anything ever again, either!"

Norcross grinned. Maybe Henry had something there.

Then, noting that the sun had just vanished, he was home.

Up in his room, Danny Norcross woke groggily from a slumber that had been full of dreams. Half asleep still, he groped for and found the little piece of ivory he had kept beside him ever since he had fallen asleep the night before.

His brow wrinkled. He had been on the stair, listening to the grown-ups talk. They had said a lot of queer things. About horses, and money, and pictures. Then he had gotten back in bed. And played with his bit of ivory for a while. Then he had had a funny thought, and sort of a wish—

The wish that had passed through his mind, as he had been falling asleep, had been that all the things Dad and Mom and the others had said would come true, because it would be so funny if they did.

So he had wished that just for one day, maybe, all Henry Jones' wishes would be horses, and money would stick to Luke Hawks' fingers, and Jacob Earl would touch something that would coin money for somebody else for a change.

And, too, that Netty Peters' tongue really would be hinged in the middle and wag at both ends, and Mrs. Benson have two faces, and Mrs. Norton swell up and blow around like a balloon.

And that Miss Wilson would really be as pretty as a picture, and you could truly hear silver bells when Miss Avery talked.

That had been his wish.

But now, wide-awake and staring out the window at a sky all red because the sun had set, he couldn't quite remember it, try as he would. . . .

*   *   *

Crouched in her darkened room, Minerva Benson felt the back of her head for the hundredth time. First with shuddering horror, then with hope, then with incredulous relief. The dreadful face was gone now.

But she would remember it, and be haunted by it forever in her dreams.

Netty Peters stared at herself in her mirror, her eyes wide and frightened. Slowly she took her hands from her throat. The queer fluttering was gone. She could talk again without that terrible voice interrupting.

But always after, when she began to speak, she would stop abruptly for fear it might sound again, in the middle of a sentence.

"I've decided, Luke," Mrs. Luke Hawks said with decision, "that we'll have the house painted and put in a new furnace. Then I'm going to take the children off on a little vacation.

"No, don't say anything! Remember, the money is in my name now, and I can spend it all, if I've a mind to. I can take it and go away to California, or anyplace.

"And no matter what you say or do, I'm not going to give it back!"

*   *   *

Jacob Earl uttered a groan. The last gold ingot had just vanished from the floor of his library.

John Wiggins turned. The tiny *clink-clink* that had sounded all afternoon had ceased. The little god still grinned, but the coins were no longer coming from his mouth.

"He's quit," the little man announced to the flushed and radiant Alice Wilson. "But we don't care. Look how much money came out of him. Why, there must be fifteen thousand dollars there!

"Alice, we'll take a trip around the world. And we'll take him back to China, where he came from. He deserves a reward."

With the red afterglow tinting the little lake beside which he had parked the car, Bill Morrow turned. His arm was already about Janice Avery's shoulders.

So it really wasn't any effort for him to draw her closer and kiss her, firmly, masterfully.

The door to Danny's room opened. He heard Dad and Mom come in, and pretended for a minute that he was asleep.

"He's been napping all day," Mom was saying. "He hardly woke up enough to eat breakfast. I guess he must have lain awake last night. But his fever was down, and he didn't seem restless, so I didn't call you."

"We'll see how he is now," Dad's voice answered; and Danny, who had closed his eyes to try to remember better, opened them again.

Dad was bending over his bed.

"How do you feel, son?" he asked.

"I feel swell," Danny told him, and struggled to a sitting position. "Look what I found yesterday in my box. What is it, Dad?"

Doctor Norcross took the piece of ivory Danny held out, and looked at it.

"I'll be darned!" he exclaimed to his wife. "Danny's found the old Chinese talisman Grandfather Jonas brought back on the last voyage of the *Yankee Star*. He gave it to me thirty years ago. Told me it had belonged to a Chinese magician.

"Its peculiar power, he said, was that if you held it tight, you could have one wish come true, providing— as the Chinese inscription on the bottom says—your mind was pure, your spirit innocent, and your motive unselfish.

"I wished on it dozens of times, but nothing ever happened. Guess it was because I was too materialistic and wished for bicycles and things.

"Here, Danny, you can keep it. But take good care of it. It's very old; even the man who gave it to Grandfather Jonas didn't know how old it was."

Danny took back the talisman.

"I made a wish, Dad," he confessed.

"So?" Dad grinned. "Did it come true?"

"I don't know," Danny admitted. "I can't remember what it was."

Dad chuckled.

"Then I guess it didn't come true," he remarked. "Never mind; you can make another. And if that one doesn't happen either, don't fret. You can keep the talisman and tell people the story. It's a good story, even if it isn't so."

Probably it wasn't so. It was certain that the next time Danny wished, nothing happened. Nor any of the times after that. So that by and by he gave up trying.

He was always a little sorry, though, that he never could remember that first wish, made when he was almost asleep.

But he never could. Not even later, when he heard people remarking how much marriage had improved Alice Wilson's appearance and how silvery Mrs. Bob Morrow's voice was.

Pat Murphy

With Four
Lean Hounds

Often we find that what we want in the end
is not what we sought at the start.

We start with a thief: slim, wiry girl with ash-gray
hair and eyes the color of the winter sky. No one knew
how old she was and no one cared. Old enough to beat;
just barely old enough to bed.

Tarsia was running from an angry baker. The loaf
tucked under her arm was still warm. She dodged
between the stalls of the market, heading for a spot
where she knew she could climb the tumble-down wall
that ringed the city. From there she could run sure-
footed across slate roofs, hide among the chimneys. A
creature of the wind and sky, she could escape all
pursuit.

She heard the whistle of the guard's warning and
the pounding of his running feet. Ill luck: he was be-

tween her and the wall. Behind her, the baker shouted curses. She changed course abruptly, ducking into the mouth of an alley and—too late—realized her mistake.

The walls were slick stone. Though she climbed like a monkey, she could not scale them. The alley's far end had been blocked by a new building. A dead end.

She heard the guard's whistle echoing down the cold stone walls and remembered the feel of the shackles on her wrist. Her bones ached in memory of the cold jail.

A jumble of papers that the wind had blown against the alley's end rustled. A rat peered out at Tarsia— a grizzled old grandfather rat who watched her with an arrogant air of unconcern, then turned tail and darted into a hole that had been hidden in the shadows. It was a dark, dank hole just the width of a small thief's shoulders.

Tarsia heard the footsteps at the mouth of the alley and, like a sensible thief with a healthy concern for her skin, she squeezed into the hole. Her shoulders scraped against the damp stone. A creature of rooftops and light, she wiggled down into the darkness.

On her belly, she groped her way forward, reminding herself that rats were only bats without wings. As a child of the rooftops she knew bats. But she could hear her heart beating in the narrow stone passage and she could not lift her head without bumping it.

She inched forward, telling herself that surely the drain let into a larger passage; it could not just get smaller and darker and damper. . . .

A cold blast of air fanned her face, carrying scents of still water, damp stone, and sewage. At last, she could raise her head. She felt a soft touch on her ankle—a tiny breeze rushing past—with only hint of fur and a long tail.

She heaved herself out of the drain into a larger space, quick and clumsy in her eagerness to move. She stepped forward in the darkness, stepped into nothing and stumbled, clutching at an edge she could not see, slipping and falling into a moment she did not remember.

A thunder of wings from the pigeons wheeling overhead, the scent of a charcoal fire—damp, dismal smell in the early morning—drifting from a chimney. The slate roof was cold beneath Tarsia's bare feet and the wind from the north cut through her thin shirt. In one hand she clutched the damp shirt she had taken from a rooftop clothesline. She was listening.

She had heard a sound—not the rattle of the latch of the door to the roof. Not the pigeons. Perhaps only the wind?

There again: a rumbling like drumbeats and a wild sweet whistling like pipes in a parade. From behind a cloud swept the chariot of the Lady of the Wind. She

brought the sunshine with her. She wore a silver cres-
cent moon on her forehead and a golden sun shone on
her breast. Ash-gray hair floated behind her like a
cape. Four lean hounds—winds of the North, South,
East, and West—ran laughing through the sky at her
side.

The Lady looked down at Tarsia with wise eyes,
smiled, and held out her hand. Tarsia reached out to
touch her.

Tarsia's head ached and her feet were cold. She
opened her eyes into darkness, leaving behind the bright
dream of a memory that had never been. Tarsia had
watched the caravan that carried tribute to the Lady
leave the city, heading north, but she had never seen
the Lady.

The hand with which Tarsia had clung to the edge
was sore and stiff; when she touched it to her lips, it
tasted of blood. She lay half in and half out of a cold
stream that tugged at her feet as it flowed past.

She could not go back, only forward. She felt her
way slowly, always keeping her hand on the wall and
always sniffing the air in hopes of scenting dust and
horses—city smells. She heard a rumbling sound ahead
that reminded her of cartwheels on cobblestones, and
she quickened her pace.

The tunnel opened into a cavern—a natural for-
mation in the rock of the Earth. Patches of fungus on

the walls glowed golden, casting a light dimmer than that of the moon.

The giant who lay in the center of the cavern was snoring with a rumbling like cartwheels. He slept in a cradle of rock, molded around him, it seemed, by the movements of his body. The air that blew past the giant, coming from the darkness beyond, carried the scents of grass and of freedom.

A giant blocked her way and she was only a small thief. She had never stolen from the house of the wizard or the stall of the herb-seller. She knew only the small spells that helped her break the protection of a household.

The giant had an enormous face—broad and earth-colored. He shifted in his sleep and Tarsia saw the chain on his ankle, bound to a bolt in the floor. The links were as thick as her leg; the rusted lock, the size of her head. She wondered who had imprisoned him and what he had done to deserve it. She tried to estimate the length of the chain and judged it long enough to allow him to catch anyone trying to sneak past.

The shifting breeze ruffled his hair and the rumbling stopped. Nostrils flared as he sampled the air. "I smell you," he said slowly. "I know your scent, witch. What do you want with me now?" He spoke as if he knew her.

Tarsia did not move. One hand rested on the rock

wall; one hand uselessly clutched her knife. The giant's eyes searched the shadows and found her.

"Ah," he said. "The same eyes, the same hair, the same scent—not the witch, but the witch's daughter." He grinned and Tarsia did not like the look in his eyes. "You were a long time in coming."

"I'm no one's daughter," she said. Giants and witches— she had no place in this. Her mother? She had no mother. "I'm just a poor thief from the city. And I want to get back."

"You can't get past me unless you free me, witch's daughter," he said.

"Free you?" She shook her head in disbelief. "How? Break the chain?"

The giant scowled. "A drop of your blood on the lock will free me. You must know that." His voice was unbelieving. "How can you hope to win your mother's throne when you don't even know . . ."

"Who is my mother?" she interrupted, her voice brittle.

"You don't know." He grinned and his voice took on the sly tone she had heard from the strong men who did not often have to be clever. "Free me and I'll tell you." He pulled his legs under him into an awkward crouch, his head bumping the cavern's ceiling. "Just one drop of blood and I'll let you go past. Even if the blood does not free me, I'll let you go."

"Even if it does not free you?" she asked warily.

"You doubt yourself so much?" He shrugged. "Even so."

She stepped forward, wary and ready to dart back to the passage. With her eyes on the crouching giant she nicked the scrape on her hand so that the blood flowed fresh and a drop fell onto the rusted lock. She backed away. The giant's eyes were fixed on the lock and on the smoke that rose from the lock, swirling around the chain.

She reached the far side of the cavern while the giant watched the lock, and from that safety she called out sharply, "Who is the witch who bound you here, giant? Keep your part of the bargain. Who . . . ?"

"There!" the giant said. With a triumphant movement, the giant tugged the chain and the lock fell free.

"Who is the witch?" Tarsia called again.

"Thank you for your help, witch's daughter." He stepped past her, into the darkness where the ceiling rose higher. "I will go now to play a part in bringing the prophecies to pass."

"But who is my mother?" she shouted. "You said you would tell me."

He grinned back over his shoulder. "Who would be strong enough to chain a son of the Earth? No one but the Lady of the Wind." He stepped away into the darkness.

"What?" Tarsia shouted in disbelief, but her voice echoed back to her. She could hear the giant striding away in the darkness and her mind was filled with the thunder of wings, with the baying of four lean hounds. She ran after the giant, knowing that she could not catch him but running in spite of that knowledge. The scent of fresh air and growing things grew stronger as she ran. "Wait," she called, but the giant was gone.

The air smelled of newly turned earth. She ran toward a bright light—sunlight of late afternoon. She could see the marks left by the giant's fingers where he had torn the rock aside and pushed his way out. His feet had ripped dark holes in the soft grass and the prints led down the rolling hills to the river that sparkled in the distance. She thought that she could see a splash in the river—tiny and far away—which could have been a giant splashing as he swam.

Sometimes stumbling, sometimes sliding in the grass, she ran down the hills, following the footprints. Ran until her legs slowed without her willing it. She trudged along the river bank as the shadows grew longer. She was heading north. The mountains lay to the north, and the Lady's court was in the mountains.

The light was failing when she stopped to rest. She sat down just for a moment. No more than that. Shivering in the chill twilight, she tumbled into a darkness deeper than the tunnels beneath the city.

*   *   *

A scent of a charcoal fire—damp dismal scent in the early morning—but Tarsia did not stand on the cold slate of the roof. The wind that carried the scent of smoke blew back her hair and the sound of wings was all around her.

She stood at the Lady's side in the chariot and the four hounds of the wind ran beside them. Far below, she saw the gray slate rooftop and the fluttering clothes on the line. Far below, the ancient towers of the city, the crumbling walls, the booths and stalls of the marketplace.

"This is your proper place, my daughter," the Lady said, her voice as soft as the summer breeze blowing through the towers. "Above the world at my side." The Lady took Tarsia's hand and the pain faded away.

Tarsia heard a rumbling—like the sound of cartwheels on a cobbled street. Far below, she saw the towers shake and a broad, earth-colored face glared up at them. Shaking off the dust of the hole from which he had emerged, the giant climbed to the top of the city wall in a few steps. He seemed larger than he had beneath the earth. He stood on top of the old stone tower and reached toward them. Tarsia cried out—fearful that the giant would catch them and drag them back to the earth. Back down to the smoke and the dust.

*   *   *

The scent of the smoke was real. Tarsia could feel the damp grass of the river bank beneath her, but she was warm. A cloth that smelled faintly of horse lay over her.

She forced her eyes open. A river bank in early morning—mist sparkling on the grass, a white horse grazing, smoke drifting from a small fire, a thin, brown-haired man dressed in travel-stained green watching her. "You're awake," he said. "How do you feel?"

Her head ached. She struggled to a sitting position, clutching the green cape that had served as her cover around her. Wary, used to the ways of the city, she mumbled, "I'll live."

He continued watching her. "You're a long way from anywhere in particular. Where are you going?" His accent matched that of traders from the south who had sometimes visited the city.

She twisted to look behind her at the hills. She could not see the city, and she wondered how far she had come in the winding tunnels. "I came from the city," she said. "I'm going away from the city." More alert now, Tarsia studied the white horse. It looked well-fed. The saddle that lay beside the animal was travel-worn, but she could tell that it was once of first quality. The cloak that covered her was finely woven of soft wool. A lute wrapped in similar cloth leaned against the saddle.

"I'm a minstrel," the man said. "I'm traveling north."

Tarsia nodded, thinking that when a person volunteered information it was generally false. No minstrel could afford a saddle like that one. She looked up into his brown eyes—noting in passing the gold ring on his hand. She knew she could trust him as a fellow thief. As far as she could trust a thief. She was not sure how far that was, since she had always preferred to work alone.

"I was planning to head north too," she said. "If you take me with you, I can help you out. I can build a fire that doesn't smoke. . . ." She looked at the smoldering fire and let her words trail off. She knew she looked small and helpless in the cloak and she hoped that her face was pale and smudged with dirt.

"I suppose I can't very well leave you here," he said, sounding a little annoyed. "I'll take you as far as the next town."

She got to her feet slowly, taking care to appear weak. But she made herself useful—poking the fire so that the sticks flamed. She toasted the bread that the minstrel pulled from his pack and melted cheese upon thick slices.

She helped him saddle the white horse. On a pretext of adjusting the saddlebags, she slipped her hand inside and found a money pouch. Swiftly, she palmed one, two, three coins—and slyly transferred them to her own pocket for later examination. Even if he only took her to the next town, she would profit by the association.

As they traveled alongside the river, she rode behind him on the horse. "How far north are you going?"

"To the mountains," he said and began to pick a tune on his lute.

"To the court of the Lady of the Wind," she guessed, then suppressed a smile when he frowned. Where else would a minstrel go in the mountains? She amended mentally; where else would a thief go? "Could I come with you?"

"Why?"

She shrugged as if reasons were not important. "I've never been to a court before. I've heard the Lady is very beautiful."

The minstrel shook his head. "Beautiful, but wicked."

"I can pay my way," Tarsia said, wondering if he would recognize the look of his own coins.

But he shook his head again and the tune he was playing changed, mellowing to music that she remembered from her childhood. She could not remember the words except for the refrain about the beautiful Lady and the four lean windhounds at her side. The Lady was the sister to the sun and daughter of the moon.

When the minstrel sang the refrain, it had a sneering, cynical tone. The lyrics were about how the Lady had bound the spirits of the Earth, the Water, and the

Fire, how she had captured the four winds and bound them in her tower, about how the world would be unhappy until the four winds were free.

"That isn't the way that I remember the song," Tarsia said when the minstrel finished.

He shrugged. "In my country, we pay the Lady no tribute. Our lands have been dry and our crops have been poor for five long years. We do not love the Lady."

Tarsia remembered the parade that was held each year in the Lady's honor when the tribute was sent. The city was noted for its silverwork, and each year, the best that the artisans had produced was sent to the mountain court. And the winds blew through the towers and brought rain for the farmers around the city walls.

Last year, at the end of a day of picking the pockets of parade spectators, Tarsia had climbed the city wall and watched from above the gate while the caravan headed north, winding between farmers' huts and green fields. On her high perch, she had been chilled by the wind—but glad to be above the crowd. The last horse in the caravan had carried a silver statuette of the Lady gazing into the distance with one hand resting on the head of a hound. Tarsia had felt a kinship with the Lady then—alone and proud, above the world.

"Why don't you pay tribute," she asked the minstrel. "Are you too poor?"

"Too proud," he said. "Our king will not allow it."

"How foolish!"

The minstrel smiled wryly. "Maybe so. The whole family is foolish, I suppose. Idealistic and stiff-necked."

"So the people of your land will die of pride."

He shook his head. "Perhaps. Perhaps not. Maybe something will happen." He sighed. "I don't know, though—the king seems inclined to rely on luck. He seems to think the prophecy will come to pass."

Tarsia frowned. "Why are you going to the Lady's court if you don't like her?"

"A minstrel doesn't worry about magic and winds." He started to play another song, as if to avoid further discussion. The notes echoed across the slow green waters of the river and the steady beat of the horse's hooves provided the rhythm. He sang about an undine, a river nymph who took a human lover, then betrayed him to the waters, letting the river rise to drown him.

Trees with long leaves trailed their branches in the water. The path twisted among the gnarled trunks. They wandered deeper into the shade and the river seemed to take the sunlight into itself, letting it sparkle in swirling eddies but never allowing it to escape. On the far side of the river, the bank rose in a fern-covered cliff, decked with flowers.

"Pretty country," Tarsia said.

"Treacherous country," said the minstrel. "If you

tried climbing the cliff you'd learn that those flowers mark loose rock, ready to give beneath your hand or tumble down on you."

At dusk, they were still in the wood and the trees all looked the same. They made camp in an inviting glen, but the tiny fire that Tarsia built seemed to cast little light. Tarsia thought she heard rustling in the trees and once, while she was toasting bread and cheese for dinner, thought she glimpsed a flicker of white in the distance over the river. She wrapped herself in the minstrel's extra cloak and curled up alone by the side of the fire.

For a moment she thought that she was in the cavern beneath the city: it was dark and cold. But the wind that beat against her face smelled of flowing water and growing things, and above her, she could see the stars. The Lady stood beside her, a proud, silent presence.

They had escaped the giant and Tarsia realized that the giant alone was no threat to the Lady. They dipped closer to the earth, and Tarsia could see the winding water of the river, glittering in the moonlight. She could see a tiny spot of light—her own fire—and she thought she could see the minstrel on the ground beside it. So far below.

She thought of him coming to the Lady's court to steal and she wished she could invite him into the chariot beside her. So cold and alone he looked, as she had felt so many times on the wall in the city of towers.

"You are above all that now," whispered the Lady at her side. "You are the daughter of the moon, sister to the sun."

The lapping of the water and the soft nickering of the horse woke her. The water sounded near, very near. She sat up and blinked at the sheen of moonlight on the water, just a few feet away from her. The horse stood at the limits of his tether, pulling away from the rising waters. Blinking again, Tarsia could see the slim figure of a woman dressed in white, standing in the water. At the sound of Tarsia's movement, the woman looked at her with mournful eyes.

She held out her hands to Tarsia and water dripped from the tips of her long fingers. Moonlight shimmered on her, just as it shimmered on the water. From her delicate wrists, silver chains which seemed to be fashioned of moonlight extended to the water.

Tarsia drew her legs away from the water, stood up and backed away. The water nymph stretched out her hands and almost reached Tarsia. The young thief could hear words in the sound of the lapping water. "Come to me, touch me, touch the river." Tarsia laid a hand on the horse, ready to vault to its back and run.

The moonlight touched a spot of darkness in the water—the minstrel's cloak. The water was around his neck and still he slept peacefully. His cloak drifted about his shoulders, moving with the water, half tangled around the tree against which he leaned. To reach the minstrel, Tarsia would have to touch the river and approach the woman of water. But no one would know if she ran away to her mother's court.

"Let me go, daughter of the moon," whispered the water. The breeze that rustled the leaves by Tarsia's head seemed to be chuckling.

"Let him go and I'll free you," Tarsia bargained desperately. "But let him go first." She did not know how to free the nymph. The watery hands reached for her and she wanted to leap onto the horse and run.

"Free me, and I will let him go," hissed the voice of the lapping water.

"But I can't . . . I don't know how. . . ."

A whisper in the night: "Give to me of yourself, daughter of the moon."

In the moonlight, Tarsia could see the minstrel's head fall back into the water and a swirl of silver bubbles rise. She stepped forward, ready to push the water nymph aside. Tarsia's eyes were wet: tears of frustration, anger, sorrow, pain. A single tear escaped, trickled down her face and fell into the river. Just one.

Tarsia grabbed the minstrel's cloak and his arm and roughly dragged him toward the river bank. At the sound of a long sigh, she looked up to see the moonlight chains on the water woman's arms fade. The nymph raised her hands to the sky in an exultant gesture and the river sighed: "Thank you, daughter of the Lady." The slim figure melted into the river, becoming one of the sparkling ripples in the current. The minstrel coughed and began to move.

Tarsia lit a fire to dry him out, draping the dry cloak over his shoulders. She did not need it for warmth. She felt strong—no longer a thief, but daughter to the Lady.

"How did you plan to get along without me to build fires?" she asked the minstrel.

He shrugged his slim shoulders beneath the cloak. "I trust to luck to get me by. Luck and destiny." His eyes were bright with reflected moonlight. "Sometimes they serve me well."

The next day's ride took them out of the river canyon into the golden foothills. A boy tending a flock of goats by the river stared at them in amazement. "No one ever comes by that path," he said.

Tarsia laughed, cheered by the sight of the mountains ahead. "We came that way."

"What about the undine?" the boy asked.

"What about the undine," she said, still laughing as they rode past. "We sent her on her way."

They walked the horse along the river's edge just past the goatherd. Ahead, they could see the buildings of a small town. The sun shone on Tarsia's face and she saw the mountains, craggy peaks where the snow never melted. "Take me with you to the Lady's court," she asked the minstrel suddenly. "I know why you're going there, and I want to come."

He looked startled. "You know. But . . ."

She laughed. "Do you think I'm half-witted? No minstrel could afford a horse like this one or a fine leather saddle. I knew you were a thief when we first met." She shook her head at the incredulous look on his face. "I know you are going to the Lady's court to steal."

"I see," he said slowly. "But if I'm a thief, why do you want to come with me?" He studied her face intently.

For a moment, she considered telling the truth. But she was city-bred, not trusting. "I want to see which of the stories about the Lady are true," she said. "Besides, I can help you." She could imagine herself at her mother's side, rewarding the minstrel with gold and jewels for bringing her there, and she smiled.

"It's a dangerous place," he said.

"If you don't take me, I will go alone," she said. "If you take me, I'll pay my way. I'll pay for tonight's lodging."

He nodded at last. "If you wish, I'll take you. But it's your choice."

The breeze whispered in the tall grass of the river bank. "The wind is encouraging us," Tarsia said.

"The wind is laughing at us," said the minstrel.

In the inn that night, Tarsia and the minstrel were

the center of a group of villagers. The boy with the goats had told what path they had followed. "You came past the undine," the innkeeper said in amazement. "How did you do it?"

Tarsia told them, leaving out only the water nymph's sigh of farewell. "So the river is free of the Lady's bond," said a sour-faced farmer. "She will not be happy." And the corners of his mouth turned up in a grim smile.

"Softly, friend," advised the innkeeper. "You would not want to be overheard. . . ."

"We live in the shadow of her rule," grumbled the farmer. "But maybe that will come to an end. My boy said he saw the footprints of a giant heading toward her court. These folks say the undine is free. Maybe the Lady . . ."

"Only one of the Lady's own blood can free the winds," interrupted the innkeeper. "And she has no children."

"They say she had a daughter once," said the minstrel quietly. "I studied the ancient stories as a student of the lute. They say that the child was captured in a battle with a neighboring city. The child was killed when the Lady would not release the winds to ransom the girl."

"And the Lady mourned for her daughter?" Tarsia added tentatively.

The crowd of villagers laughed and the minstrel raised his eyebrows. "I doubt it. But the stories don't really say."

A loose shutter banged in the rising wind outside the inn. The group of villagers that had gathered around Tarsia while she had been telling of the water nymph dispersed to other tables.

"Some say that the winds that the Lady allows to blow carry tales back to her," the minstrel told Tarsia softly. "No one knows for certain." The shutter banged again and the conversations around them stopped for a moment, then resumed in hushed tones.

"The land here was green once," said the minstrel. "The people have become bitter as the land has become dry."

The minstrel began to pick the notes of a slow, sweet tune, and Tarsia went to the bar to bargain with the innkeeper for their night's lodging. She took one of the minstrel's coins from her pocket and it flashed silver in the firelight. The innkeeper weighed it in his hand and turned it over to examine both sides.

"A coin of the south," he said, then peered more closely at the profile etched on one side.

The notes of the song that the minstrel was playing drifted across the room, over the sounds of conversation. He was picking out the sad ballad about the Lady that he had played the day before. The innkeeper glanced at him sharply, then looked back at the coin. He seemed to be listening to the sound of the wind prowling around the windows.

"You are heading into the mountains from here?" he asked.

"Yes," Tarsia said cautiously. She knew that he was no friend of the Lady.

He handed her back the coin. "Good luck," he said. "Eat supper as you like, and you may sleep in the loft above the stable."

She frowned at him without comprehension. "What do you mean? Why?"

He seemed to study the minstrel's face in the dim light. "Consider it as payment for ridding the river of the undine." He smiled at her for the first time, and took her hand to fold her fingers around the coin. "Good luck."

She pocketed the coin and returned unhappily to the minstrel's side. She did not like bargains she did not understand. Like the giant, the innkeeper seemed to think that she knew more than she did.

"Did you make a deal?" the minstrel asked.

She sat down on the bench beside him, frowning. "We're sleeping in the stable loft. No payment—he didn't even argue."

"I see." The minstrel nodded across the room to the innkeeper and the older man waved back, a gesture that was almost a salute.

"There are things on which one does not bargain, little one," said the minstrel. "You'll have to learn that."

That night they bedded down in sweet-smelling hay. Outside, the wind bayed like a pack of hounds on the shunt, and Tarsia lay awake. She listened to the minstrel's steady breathing and thought about the mountains and the court of the Lady. But she did not want to sleep and dream.

When she turned restlessly in the hay, the minstrel blinked at her. "Lie down and go to sleep."

"I can't," she grumbled back, into the darkness that smelled of horses.

"What's wrong?" he asked.

"I'm cold," she said, and it was true—even with his extra cloak around her, she was shivering.

He raised himself on one elbow wearily, and lifted his cloak to invite her to lie beside him. She snuggled against his chest and he touched her cheek lightly. "What's worrying you?" he asked. "Do you want to turn back?"

"It used to be so simple," she said, half to herself. "I used to be just a thief in the city, climbing on the city wall and laughing at people who were foolish enough to let me pick their pockets. So simple. . . ."

"What are you now?" Though his voice was soft, the question had edges.

The winds bayed and she shivered. "No one. No one at all."

The minstrel rocked her gently in his arms and she

listened to his steady breathing as he slept beside her. She slept, but not easily.

The Lady's hand was warm on Tarsia's. Far below, the small thief could see the village: toy huts set on a golden hillside. The mountains rose ahead of them: cold, gray, and forbidding.

"We don't need them," the Lady said in her soft voice. "It doesn't matter that they hate me."

The wind was in Tarsia's face and the stars wheeled about her and she was high above them all. No one could touch her here. No one could put her in shackles or chase her into the sewers. She had come home.

She was quiet when they left town the next morning. The same boy who had met them on the river path was grazing his goats on the hillside. "There are robbers in the mountains," he called to them. "They'll get you if you go up there." The boy was cheerful at the prospect. "There's a dragon, too. The Lady bound him there. If the robbers don't get you, the dragon will find you and . . ."

The minstrel urged the horse through the center of the boy's herd and the goats scattered, bleating as they ran.

The horse picked its way carefully up the dry slopes. Toward dusk, the grass gave way to rough rock and the animal began stumbling in the dying light. At Tarsia's suggestion, they dismounted and led the horse. To shake the saddle-weariness from her legs, Tarsia ran ahead, dodging around rocks and scrambling up boulders, feeling almost as if she were at home on the walls of the city. She climbed a rock face and peered over the edge at the minstrel, considering surprising him from above. She saw a movement—a flash of brown—on the trail ahead of him, movements in the brush on either side.

"Hold it there." The man who stepped from behind a boulder had an arrow pointed at the minstrel. Other men closed in from behind.

"I have nothing of value," said the minstrel casually. "Nothing at all."

"You've got a horse," said the leader of the robbers. The man had a soft, lilting accent like the minstrel's. "And I think we need it more than you do." The man lifted the minstrel's money pouch from his belt. Grinning, he hefted the pouch in his hand and gazed at the minstrel's face. "Damn, but your face looks familiar. Do I know you . . . ?" His voice trailed off.

"I'm going to the court of the Lady. I need the horse to get there," the minstrel said.

"A man of the south going to visit the Lady," the leader wondered. "Strange. Since our foolish king has refused to pay tribute to the Lady, few from the south venture into her mountains." As he spoke, he fumbled with the minstrel's pouch, pouring a stream of coins into his hand. "Nothing of value," he said then. "Just pretty gold and silver." The robber held a coin up to the light of the dying sun—just as the innkeeper had held it up—and he whistled long and low. He glanced at the minstrel's face and Tarsia could see his teeth flash in a grin. "Did I say our king was foolish? Not so foolish as his son." The leader tossed the coin to another man in the circle. "Look. We've got a prince here."

The coin was tossed from hand to hand—each man inspecting the minstrel and the coin, the coin and the minstrel. Tarsia, peering over the edge, tried to remember the profile on the coin, briefly glimpsed in a dim light. She tugged a coin from her pocket and compared the cold metal etching with the minstrel's face. They matched.

"We follow our destiny and our luck," the minstrel—or the prince?—was saying. "I am on a mission at my father's request."

The leader's grin broadened and he tossed a coin into the air so that it flashed gold as it tumbled back to his hand. "Bringing tribute," the leader said.

"No." The winds were silent and the voice of the prince—once, the minstrel—was calm. "I have come to free the winds."

Tarsia leaned against the rock and listened to the rhythm of her heart—beating faster and faster. She

Young Witches & Warlocks

heard the leader laugh. "What do you expect the Lady to say to that?"

"I may have to destroy the Lady. But the winds must be free. For the sake of the land you have left behind, you must let me go."

"You appeal to the honor of a thief?" the leader said. "You are foolish indeed. And foolish to think that you alone can destroy our Lady."

The prince looked up then, just as if he had known all along where Tarsia was hidden, then looked back to the leader. But his words were echoing in Tarsia's mind: "destroy the Lady . . ." And in her mind, the winds howled. The prince was not alone; the giant had been seen climbing toward her court and the undine was free. Tarsia leaned against the rock for support and listened to the men argue about what to do with the minstrel—no, the prince. She had to remind herself he was a prince. They could hold him for ransom, deliver him to the Lady for a reward, kill him on the spot, feed him to the dragon. She followed, a little above them and a little behind them as they walked to the dragon's cave, still arguing. She heard the horse nicker softly as they stood at the cave entrance. The man who held the animal's reins was right below her hiding place, paying more attention to the argument than to the horse.

Tarsia sprang. Landed half on and half off the white horse's broad back, gripping its mane and pounding

its sides with her heels. The animal leaped forward—
was it by the horse's inclination or her direction? she
was not sure—toward the prince. The horse reared as
she strove to turn it, dancing in place and throwing
its head back, startled past the capacity of even a well-
trained horse to bear. Tarsia fought for control, only
partly aware of the men who dodged away from the
animal's hooves in the dim light of twilight. She could
not see the prince.

A crackling of flame, a scent of sulfur, and the mountain was no longer dark. Small thief—she had never
dabbled in magic, never met a dragon. If she had imagined anything, she had imagined a lizard breathing fire.

A lightning bolt, a fireworks blast, a bonfire—but
it moved like an animal. Where it stepped, it left cinders and when it lifted its head she stared into the
white glory of its eyes. A sweep of its tail left a trail
of sparks. Half flame, half animal—or perhaps more
than half flame.

She could see the prince, standing in its path. The
child of fire opened its mouth and for a moment she
could see the jagged lightning of its teeth.

"Child of fire," Tarsia called to it. "If I free you will
you lead me to my mother?"

The crackling warmth assented with a burst of heat
and a flare of flame.

Tarsia's heart was large within her and she was
caught by confusion—burning with shame and stung

by betrayal. She saw the prince through a haze of smoke and anger. The coins she had stolen from him were in her hand and she wanted to be rid of them and rid of him. "I give of myself to you, child of fire." she said, and hurled them into the flames. Three points of gold, suddenly molten.

The heat of her pain vanished with them. She burned pure and cold—like starlight, like moonlight, like a reflection from the heart of an icicle.

The dragon beat his wings and she felt a wave of heat. He circled the mountain, caught an updraft and soared higher. His flame licked out and lashed the granite slope beneath him before he rose out of sight.

In the sudden silence, Tarsia fought the horse to a standstill. The prince stood alone by the cave. The world was tinted with the transparent twilight blue of early evening in the mountains, touched with smoke and sprinkled with snow.

"You didn't tell me you wanted to free the winds," Tarsia said. Her voice still carried the power it had had when she spoke to the dragon. "You didn't tell me you were a prince."

"I could only trust you as much as you could trust me, daughter of the wind."

"Ah, you know." Her voice was proud.

"I guessed. You freed the undine," he said.

"Had you planned to use me to destroy my mother?" she asked. "That won't work, prophecy or no. I'm here to help my mother, not to destroy her." She urged the horse up the canyon, following the mark left by the dragon's fire. She did not look back.

Up the mountains, following the trail of burnt brush and cinders, kicking the horse when it stumbled, urging it to run over grassy slopes marked by flame. The moon rose and the horse stumbled less often. Alpine flowers nodded in the wind of her passing and on the snow banks, ice crystals danced in swirling patterns.

The towers of the Lady's castle rose from the center of a bowl carved into the mountain. A wall of ice rose behind the towers—glacial blue in the moonlight. The ice had been wrought with tunnels by the wind and carved into strangely shaped pillars. Tarsia rode over the crest of the ridge and started the horse down the slope toward the gates when she saw the giant by the towers.

She felt the strength within her, and did not turn.

As Tarsia drew nearer she saw the figure in the ice wall—the slim form of the undine. She smelled the reek of sulfur and the ice flickered red as the dragon circled the towers.

The gates had been torn from their hinges. The snow had drifted into the courtyard. The stones had been scorched by fire.

Tarsia pulled the horse to a stop in front of the grinning giant. "So you've come to finish the job," he said.

"I have come to see my mother," Tarsia answered, her voice cold and careful.

"I hope you know more than you did when I talked to you last," said the giant.

"I have come to talk to my mother," she repeated. "What I know or what I plan to do is none of your concern." Her voice was cold as starlight.

The giant frowned. "Your mother's men have fled. Her castle is broken. But still she holds the winds in her power. She stands there where we cannot follow." The giant gestured to the tallest tower. Tarsia noticed that the wind had scoured a bare spot in the snow at the tower's base. "Visit her if you will."

Tarsia left the white horse standing by the tower door and climbed the cold stairs alone. She could feel a breeze tickling the back of her neck and tugging at her clothes. She was cold, so cold, as cold as she had been the morning she stole the loaf of bread.

A slender figure was silhouetted in the doorway against the sky. "So you have come to destroy me," said a voice that was at the same time silky and sharp.

"No," Tarsia protested. "Not to destroy you. I came to help you."

She looked up into the gray eyes. The Lady was as beautiful as Tarsia's vision: slim, gray-eyed, ashen haired, dressed in a gown as white as a cloud. In her hand, she held on leash four hounds. They were silver in the moonlight and their bodies seemed to shimmer.

Their eyes were pools of darkness and Tarsia wondered what the winds of the world thought about.
Where would they wander if they were not on leash?
The breeze tugged at her hair and she wondered why
they needed to be bound.

Tarsia stared into the Lady's eyes and the lady
laughed—a sound like icicles breaking in the wind. "I
see myself in your eyes, daughter. You have come to
help." She reached out and touched the girl's shoulder,
pulling the young thief to her. Her hand was cold—
Tarsia could feel its chill to her bones.

The wind beat in Tarsia's face as she stood beside
the Lady, looking down at the giant and the snowbank,
silvered by moonlight. The dragon swooped down to
land nearby and the glow of his flames lent a ruddy
cast to the snow.

"We are above them, daughter," said the Lady. "We
don't need them."

Tarsia did not speak. Looking down, Tarsia saw the
piece of chain still dangling from the giant's arm and
remembered wondering why he had been bound.

"You are waiting for the coming of the one who will
destroy me?" called the Lady. "You will wait forever.
Here she stands. My daughter has joined me and we
will be stronger together than I was alone. You will
be cast back to your prisons."

The dragon raised its fiery wings in a blaze of glory.
The giant stood by the gate, broad face set in a scowl.

The undine flowed from one ice pillar to another—her body distorted by the strange shapes through which she passed.

"All who have risen against me will be chained," said the Lady.

"That need not be," said Tarsia, her voice small compared to her mother's. Then she called out to the three who waited, "Will you promise never to attack us again? Will you vow to . . ."

"Daughter, there can be no bargains," said the Lady. "No deals, no vows, no promises. You must learn. Those who betray you must be punished. You have power over them; you cannot bargain with them."

The Lady's voice gained power as she spoke—the cold force of a winter wind. Not angry, it was cold, bitter cold. Like the bitter wind that had wailed around the towers of the city—alone, lonely, proud. Like the gusts that had chilled Tarsia when she slept on the city wall. Like the chill in the dungeon when she was chained and unable to escape.

Tarsia looked at the hounds at her mother's feet: shimmering sleek hounds with eyes of night. Why must they be chained? She looked at the Lady: sculpted of ivory, her hair spun silver in the moonlight.

"Go," Tarsia told the hounds. "Be free." The words left her body like a sigh. And the power that would have been hers, that had been hers for a time, left her with the breath. With her sharp knife and an ease born of a magic she did not understand, she reached out and slashed the leashes that held the hounds. Beneath her, the tower trembled.

The hounds leaped forward, laughing now, tongues lolling over flashing teeth, sleek legs hurling them into the air, smiling hounds looking less like hounds and more like ghosts, like silver sand blown by the wind. The Lady's hair whirled about her. She lifted white arms over her head, reaching out to the faraway moon. Tarsia watched and knew that she would never be so beautiful, never be so powerful, never would the winds heel to her command.

The tower trembled and the scent of sulfur was all around and crystals of snow beat at Tarsia's face. She felt herself lifted—or thrown and caught and tumbled like a coin through the air.

Somehow, someone shut out the moon and stars.

A scent of a charcoal fire—damp dismal smell in the early morning—and . . . damn, she thought. Will I never be free of this? She forced her eyes open.

"You're awake," said the prince. "How do you feel?"

She had been angry, she remembered. And she had been cold with a frozen bitterness. Now she felt only an emptiness where once the power had dwelled within her. She felt empty and light.

She looked back at her mother's castle. A ruin: scorched stones marked with the handprints of the giant, dusted with snow and tumbled by the wind. The ice had crept over the ruin, cracking some stones. Tarsia shivered.

She struggled to her feet and stepped away from the castle, toward the village. Ahead, she could see snow crystals whirling on the surface of a drift. The grass around her feet shifted restlessly in the breeze. She looked at the prince and thought of all the things that she wanted to explain or ask—but she did not speak. The wind flirted with the hem of her skirt and tickled the back of her neck.

"I'll take you with me to my land if you bring the winds along," the prince said. His gaze was steady, regarding her as an equal.

"I can't bring them," she said. "I am not their mistress."

"They will follow," said the prince. "You're their friend."

The breeze helped him wrap his cape around her and the winds made the flowers dance as the prince and the thief rode away from the ruins.

William Tenn

Mistress Sary

It was a particular talent Sarietta had . . .
to get others hot under the collar.

This evening, as I was about to enter my home, I saw
two little girls bouncing a ball solemnly on the pave-
ment to the rhythm of a very old little girls' chant. My
lips must have gone gray as the sudden pressure of
my set jaws numbed all feeling, blood pounded in my
right temple; and I knew that, whatever might happen, I couldn't take another step until they had finished.

> *One, two, three alary—*
> *I spy Mistress Sary*
> *Sitting on a bumble-ary,*
> *Just like a little fairy!*

As the girl finished the last smug note, I came to
life. I unlocked the door of my house and locked it

behind me hurriedly. I switched on the lights in the foyer, the kitchen, the library. And then, for long forgotten minutes, I paced the floor until my breathing slowed and the horrible memory cowered back into the crevice of the years.

That verse! I don't hate children—no matter what my friends say, I don't hate children—but why do they have to sing that stupid little song? Whenever I'm around. . . . As if the unspeakably vicious creatures know what it does to me. . . .

Sarietta Hawn came to live with Mrs. Clayton when her father died in the West Indies. Her mother had been Mrs. Clayton's only sister, and her father, a British colonial administrator, had no known relatives. It was only natural that the child should be sent across the Caribbean to join my landlady's establishment in Nanville. It was natural, too, that she should be enrolled in the Nanville Grade School where I taught arithmetic and science to the accompaniment of Miss Drury's English, history and geography.

"That Hawn child is impossible, unbelievable!" Miss Drury stormed into my classroom at the morning recess. "She's a freak, an impudent, ugly little freak!"

I waited for the echoes to die down in the empty classroom and considered Drury's intentional Victorian figure with amusement. Her heavily corseted bosom heaved and the thick skirts and petticoats slapped against her ankles as she walked feverishly in front of my desk. I leaned back and braced my arms against my head.

"Now you better be careful. I've been very busy for the past two weeks with a new term and all, and I haven't had a chance to take a good look at Sarietta. Mrs. Clayton doesn't have any children of her own, though, and since the girl arrived on Thursday the woman has been falling all over her with affection. She won't stand for punishing Sarietta like—well, like you did Joey Richards last week. Neither will the school board for that matter."

Miss Drury tossed her head angrily. "When you've been teaching as long as I have, young man, you'll learn that sparing the rod just does not work with stubborn brats like Joey Richards. He'll grow up to be the same kind of no-account drunk as his father if I don't give him a taste of birch now and then."

"All right. Just remember that several members of the school board are beginning to watch you very closely. Now what's this about Sarietta Hawn being a freak? She's an albino, as I recall; lack of pigmentation is due to a chance factor of heredity, not at all freakish, as is experienced by thousands of people who lead normal happy lives."

"Heredity!" A contemptuous sniff. "More of that new nonsense. She's a freak, I tell you, as nasty a little devil as Satan ever made. When I asked her to tell the class about her home in the West Indies, she stood up and squeaked, 'That is a book closed to fools and simpletons.' Well! If the recess bell hadn't rung at that moment, I tell you I'd have laced into her right then and there."

She glanced down at her watch pendant. "Recess almost over. You'd better have the bell system checked, Mr. Flynn: I think it rang a minute too early this morning. And don't allow that Hawn child to give you any sass."

"None of the children ever do." I grinned as the door slammed behind her.

A moment later there was laughter and chatter as the room filled with eight-year-olds.

I began my lesson on long division with a covert glance at the last row. Sarietta Hawn sat stiffly there, her hands neatly clasped on the desk. Against the mahogany veneer of the classroom furniture, her long, ashen pigtails and absolutely white skin seemed to acquire a yellowish tinge. Her eyes were slightly yellow, too, great colorless irises under semitransparent lids that never blinked while I looked at her.

She *was* an ugly child. Her mouth was far too generous for beauty; her ears stood out almost at right angles to her head; and the long tip of her nose had an odd curve down and in to her upper lip. She wore a snow-white frock of severe cut that added illogical years to her thin body.

When I finished the arithmetic lesson, I walked up

to the lonely little figure in the rear. "Wouldn't you like to sit a little closer to my desk?" I asked in as gentle a voice as I could. "You'd find it easier to see the blackboard."

She rose and dropped a swift curtsy. "I thank you very much, sir, but the sunlight at the front of the classroom hurts my eyes. There is always more comfort for me in darkness and in shade." The barest, awkward flash of a grateful smile.

I nodded, feeling uncomfortable at her formal, correct sentences.

During the science lesson, I felt her eyes upon me wherever I moved. I found myself fumbling at the equipment under that unwinking scrutiny, and the children, sensing the cause, began to whisper and crane their necks to the back of the room.

A case of mounted butterflies slid out of my hands. I stopped to pick it up. Suddenly a great gasp rippled over the room, coming simultaneously from thirty little throats.

"Look! She's doing it again!" I straightened.

Sarietta Hawn hadn't moved from her strange, stiff position. But her hair was a rich chestnut now; her eyes were blue; her cheeks and lips bore a delicate rose tint.

My fingers dug into the unyielding surface of my desk. Impossible! Yet could light and shade play such fantastic tricks? But—impossible!

Even as I gaped, unconscious of my pedagogical dignity, the child seemed to blush and a shadow over her straighten. I went back to cocoons and *Lepidoptera* with a quavering voice.

A moment later, I noticed that her face and hair were of purest white once more. I wasn't interested in explanation, however; neither was the class. The lesson was ruined.

"She did exactly the same thing in my class," Miss Drury exclaimed at lunch. "Exactly the same thing! Only it seemed to me that she was a dark brunette, with velvet black hair and snapping black eyes. It was just after she'd called me a fool—the nerve of that snip!—and I was reaching for the birch rod, when she seemed to go all dark and swarthy. I'd have made her change to red though, I can tell you, if that bell hadn't rung a minute too early."

"Maybe," I said. "But with that sort of delicate coloring any change in lighting would play wild tricks with your vision. I'm not so sure that I saw it after all. Sarietta Hawn is no chameleon."

The old teacher tightened her lips until they were a pale, pink line cutting across her wrinkled face. She shook her head and leaned across the crumb-bespattered table. "No chameleon. A witch. I know! And the Bible commands us to destroy witches, to burn them out of life."

My laugh echoed uncomfortably around the dirty school basement which was our lunchroom. "You can't believe that! An eight-year-old girl—"

"All the more reason to catch her before she grows up and does real harm. I tell you, Mr. Flynn, I know! One of my ancestors burned thirty witches in New England during the trials. My family has a special sense for the creatures. There can be no peace between us!"

The other children shared an awed agreement with Miss Drury. They began calling the albino child "Mistress Sary." Sarietta, on the other hand, seemed to relish the nickname. When Joey Richards tore into a group of children who were following her down the street and shouting the song, she stopped him.

"Leave them alone, Joseph," she warned him in her curious adult phraseology. "They are quite correct: I *am* just like a little fairy."

And Joey turned his freckled, puzzled face and unclenched his fists and walked slowly back to her side. He worshiped her. Possibly because of two of them were outcasts in that juvenile community, possibly because they were both orphans—his eternally soused father was slightly worse than no parent at all—they were always together. I'd find him squatting at her feet in the humid twilight when I came out on the boarding-house porch for my nightcap of fresh air. She would pause in mid-sentence, one tiny forefinger still poised sharply. Both of them would sit in absolute silence until I left the porch.

Joey liked me a little. Thus I was one of the few privileged to hear of Mistress Sary's earlier life. I turned one evening when I was out for a stroll to see Joey trotting behind me. He had just left the porch.

"Gee," he sighed. "Stogolo sure taught Mistress Sary a lot. I wish that guy was around to take care of Old Dreary. He'd teach her all right, all right."

"Stogolo?"

"Sure. He was the witch-doctor who put the devil-birth curse on Sary's mother before Sary was born 'cause she had him put in jail. Then when Sary's mother died giving birth, Sary's father started drinking, she says, worse'n my pop. Only she found Stogolo and made friends with him. They mixed blood and swore peace on the grave of Sary's mother. And he taught her voodoo an' the devil-birth curse an' how to make love charms from hog liver an'—"

"I'm surprised at you, Joey," I interrupted. "Taking in that silly superstition! A boy who does as well as you in science! Mistress Sary—Sarietta grew up in a primitive community where people didn't know any better. But you do!"

He scuffed the weeds at the edge of the sidewalk with a swinging foot. "Yeah," he said in a low voice. "Yeah. I'm sorry I mentioned it, Mr. Flynn."

Then he was off, a lithe streak in white blouse and corduroy knickers, tearing along the sidewalk to his home. I regretted my interruption, then, since Joey was rarely confidential and Sarietta spoke only when spoken to, even with her aunt.

The weather grew surprisingly warmer. "I declare," Miss Drury told me one morning, "I've never seen a winter like this in my life. Indian summers and heat waves are one thing, but to go on this way day after day without any sign of a break, land sakes!"

"Scientists say the entire earth is developing a warmer climate. Of course, it's almost imperceptible right now, but the Gulf Stream—"

"The Gulf Stream," she ridiculed. She wore the same starched and heavy clothes as always and the heat was reducing her short temper to a blazing point. "The Gulf Stream! Ever since that Hawn brat came to live in Nanville the world's been turning turtle. My chalk is always breaking, my desk drawers get stuck, the erasers fall apart—the little witch is trying to put a spell on me!"

"Now look here." I stopped and faced her with my back to the school building. "This has gone far enough. If you do have to believe in witchcraft, keep it out of your relations with the children. They're here to absorb knowledge, not the hysterical imaginings of a— of a—"

"Of a sour old maid. Yes, go ahead, say it," she

snarled. "I know you think it, Mr. Flynn. You fawn all over her so she leaves you be. But I know what I know and so does the evil little thing you call Sarietta Hawn. It's war between us, and the all-embracing battle between good and evil will never be over until one or the other of us is dead!" She turned in a spiral of skirts and swept up the path into the schoolhouse.

I began to fear for her sanity then. I remembered her boast: "I've never read a novel published after 1893!"

That was the day my arithmetic class entered slowly, quietly as if a bubble of silence enveloped them. The moment the door shut behind the last pupil, the bubble broke and whispers splattered all over the room.

"Where's Sarietta Hawn?" I asked. "And Joey Richards," I amended, unable to find him either.

Louise Bell rose, her starched pink dress curving in front of her scrawny body. "They've been naughty. Miss Drury caught Joey cutting a lock of hair off her head and she started to whip him. Then Mistress Sary stood up and said she wasn't to touch him because he was under her pro-tec-tion. So Miss Drury sent us all out and now I bet she's going to whip them both. She's real mad!"

I started for the back door rapidly. Abruptly a scream began. Sarietta's voice! I tore down the corridor. The scream rose to a high treble, wavered for a second. Then stopped.

As I jolted open the door of Miss Drury's classroom, I was prepared for anything, including murder. I was not prepared for what I saw. I stood, my hand grasping the door knob, absorbing the tense tableau.

Joey Richards was backed against the blackboard, squeezing a long tendril of brownish hair in his sweaty right palm. Mistress Sary stood in front of Miss Drury, her head bent to expose a brutal red welt on the back of her chalky neck. And Miss Drury was looking stupidly at a fragment of birch in her hand; the rest of the rod lay in scattered pieces at her feet.

The children saw me and came to life. Mistress Sary straightened and with set lips moved toward the door. Joey Richards leaned forward. He rubbed the lock of hair against the back of the teacher's dress, she completely oblivious to him. When he joined the girl at the door, I saw that the hair glistened with the perspiration picked up from Miss Drury's blouse.

At a slight nod from Mistress Sary, the boy passed the lock of hair over to her. She placed it very carefully in the pocket of her frock.

Then, without a single word, they both skipped around me on their way to join the rest of the class.

Evidently they were unharmed, at least seriously.

I walked over to Miss Drury. She was trembling violently and talking to herself. She never removed her eyes from the fragment of birch.

"It just flew to pieces. Flew to pieces! I was—when it flew to pieces!"

Placing an arm about her waist, I guided the spinster to a chair. She sat down and continued mumbling.

"Once—I just struck her once. I was raising my arm for another blow—the birch was over my head—when it flew to pieces. Joey was off in a corner—he couldn't have done it—the birch just flew to pieces." She stared at the piece of wood in her hand and rocked her body back and forth slowly, like one mourning a great loss.

I had a class. I got her a glass of water, notified the janitor to take care of her and hurried back.

Somebody, in a childish spirit of ridicule or meanness, had scrawled a large verse across the blackboard in my room:

> *One, two, three alary—*
> *I spy Mistress Sary*
> *Sitting on a bumble-ary,*
> *Just like a little fairy!*

I turned angrily to the class. I noticed a change in seating arrangements. Joey Richards' desk was empty.

He had taken his place with Mistress Sary in the long, deep shadows at the back of the room.

To my breathless relief, Mistress Sary didn't mention the incident. As always she was silent at the supper table, her eyes fixed rigidly on her plate. She excused herself the moment the meal was over and slipped away. Mrs. Clayton was evidently too bustling and talkative to have heard of it. There would be no repercussions from that quarter.

After supper I walked over to the old-fashioned gabled house where Miss Drury lived with her relatives. Lakes of perspiration formed on my body and I found it all but impossible to concentrate. Every leaf on every tree hung motionless in the humid, breezeless night.

The old teacher was feeling much better. But she refused to drop the matter; to do, as I suggested, her best to reestablish amity. She rocked herself back and forth in great scoops of the colonial rocking chair and shook her head violently.

"No, no, *no*! I won't make friends with that imp of darkness: sooner shake hands with Beelzebub himself. She hates me now worse than ever because—don't you see—I forced her to declare herself. I've made her expose her witchery. Now—now I must grapple with her and overthrow her and Him who is her mentor. I must think, I must—only it's so devilishly hot. So very hot! My mind—my mind doesn't seem to work right." She wiped her forehead with the heavy cashmere shawl.

As I strolled back, I fumbled unhappily for a solution. Something would break soon at this rate; then the school board would be down upon us with an investigation and the school would go to pot. I tried to go over the possibilities calmly but my clothes stuck to my body and breathing was almost drudgery.

Our porch was deserted. I saw movement in the garden and hurried over. Two shadows resolved into Mistress Sary and Joey Richards. They stared up as if waiting for me to declare myself.

She was squatting on the ground and holding a doll in her hands. A small wax doll with brownish hair planted in her head that was caught in a stern bun just like the bun Miss Drury affected. A stiff little doll with a dirty piece of muslin for a dress cut in the same long, severe pattern as all of Miss Drury's clothes. A carefully executed caricature in wax.

"Don't you think that's a bit silly," I managed to ask at last. "Miss Drury is sufficiently upset and sorry for what she did for you to play upon her superstitions in this horrible way. I'm sure if you try hard enough, we can all be friends."

They rose, Sarietta clutching the doll to her breast. "It is not silly, Mr. Flynn. That bad woman must be taught a lesson. A terrible lesson she will never forget. Excuse my abruptness, sir, but I have much work to do this night."

And then she was gone, a rustling patch of whiteness that slipped up the stairs and disappeared into the sleeping house.

I turned to the boy.

"Joey, you're a pretty smart fellow. Man to man, now—"

"Excuse me, Mr. Flynn." He started for the gate. "I—I got to go home." I heard the rhythmic pad of his sneakers on the sidewalk grow faint and dissolve in the distance. I had evidently lost his allegiance.

Sleep came hard that night. I tossed on entangling sheets, dozed, came awake and dozed again.

About midnight, I woke shuddering. I punched the pillow and was about to attempt unconsciousness once more when my ears caught a faint note of sound. I recognized it. That was what had reached into my dreams and tugged my eyes open to fear. I sat upright.

Sarietta's voice!

She was singing a song, a rapid song with unrecognizable words. Higher and higher up the scale it went, and faster and faster as if there were some eerie deadline she had to meet. At last, when it seemed that she would shrill beyond the limits of human audibility, she paused. Then, on a note so high that my ear drums ached, came a drawn-out, flowing "Kurunoo O Stogoloooo!"

Silence.

Two hours later, I managed to fall asleep again.

The sun burning redly through my eyelids wakened me. I dressed, feeling oddly listless and apathetic. I wasn't hungry and, for the first morning of my life, went without breakfast.

The heat came up from the sidewalk and drenched my face and hands. My feet felt the burning concrete through the soles of my shoes. Even the shade of the school building was an unnoticeable relief.

Miss Drury's appetite was gone too. She left her carefully wrapped lettuce sandwiches untouched on the basement table. She supported her head on her thin hands and stared at me out of red-rimmed eyes.

"It's so hot!" she whispered. "I can hardly stand it. Why everyone feels so sorry for that Hawn brat, I can't understand. Just because I made her sit in the sunlight. I've been suffering from this heat a thousand times more than she."

"You . . . made—Sarietta . . . sit—in—"

"Of course I did! She's no privileged character. Always in the back of the room where it's cool and comfortable. I made her change her desk so that she's right near the large window, where the sunlight streams in. And she feels it too, let me tell you. Only—ever since, I've been feeling worse. As if I'm falling apart. I didn't have a wink of sleep last night—those terrible, terrible dreams: great hands pulling and mauling me, knives pricking my face and my hands—"

"But the child can't stand sunlight! She's an albino."

"Albino, fiddlesticks! She's a witch. She'll be making wax dolls next. Joey Richards didn't try to cut my hair for a joke. He had orders to— Ooh!" She doubled in her chair. "Those cramps!"

I waited until the attack subsided and watched her sweaty, haggard face. "Funny that you should mention wax dolls. You have the girl so convinced that she's a witch that she's actually making them. Believe it or not, last night, after I left you—"

She had jumped to her feet and was rigid attention. One arm supporting her body against a steam pipe, she stood staring at me.

"She made a wax doll. Of me?"

"Well, you know how a child is. It was her idea of what you looked like. A little crude in design, but a good piece of workmanship. Personally, I think her talent merits encouragement."

Miss Drury hadn't heard me. "Cramps!" she mused. "And I thought they were cramps! She's been sticking pins into me! The little— I've got to— But I must be careful. Yet fast. Fast."

I got to my feet and tried to put my hand on her shoulder across the luncheon table. "Now pull yourself together. Surely this is going altogether too far."

She leaped away and stood near the stairs talking rapidly to herself. "I can't use a stick or a club—she controls them. But my hands—if I can get my hands on her and choke fast enough, she can't stop me. But I mustn't give her a chance," she almost sobbed, "*I mustn't give her a chance!*"

Then she had leaped up the stairs in a sudden, determined rush.

I swept the table out of my way and bolted after her.

Most of the children were eating their lunches along the long board fence at the end of the school yard. But they had stopped now and were watching something with frightened fascination. Sandwiches hung suspended in front of open mouths. I followed the direction of their stares.

Miss Drury was slipping along the side of the building like an upright, skirted panther. She staggered now and then and held on to a wall. Some two feet in front of her, Sarietta Hawn and Joey Richards sat in the shade. They were looking intently at a wax doll in a muslin dress that had been set on the cement just outside the fringe of coolness. It lay on its back in the direct sunlight and, even at that distance, I could see it was melting.

"Hi," I shouted. "Miss Drury! Be sensible!" I ran for them.

At my cry, both children looked up, startled. Miss Drury launched herself forward and fell, rather than leaped, on the little girl. Joey Richards grabbed the doll and rolled out of the way toward me. I tripped over him and hit the ground with a bone-breaking wallop. As I turned in midair, I caught a fast glimpse of Miss Drury's right hand flailing over the girl. Sarietta had huddled into a pathetic little bundle under the teacher's body.

I sat up facing Joey. Behind me the children were screaming as I had never heard them scream before.

Joey was squeezing the doll with both hands. As I watched, not daring to remove my eyes, the wax— already softened by the sunlight—lost its shape and came through the cracks in his tight freckled fingers. It dripped through the muslin dress and fell in blobs on the school yard cement.

Over and above the yells of the children, Miss Drury's voice rose to an agony-filled scream and went on and on and on.

Joey looked over my shoulder with rolling eyes. But he kept on squeezing the doll and I kept my eyes on it desperately, prayerfully, while the screaming went on all about me and the intense sun pushed the perspiration steadily down my face. As the wax oozed through his fingers, he began singing suddenly in a breathless, hysterical cackle.

> *One, two, three alary—*
> *I spy Mistress Sary*
> *Sitting on a bumble-ary,*
> *Just like a little fairy!*

And Miss Drury screamed and the children yelled and Joey sang, but I kept my eyes on the little wax doll. *I kept my eyes on the little wax doll drooling through the cracks of Joey Richards' strained, little fingers. I kept my eyes on the doll.*

Evelyn E. Smith

Teragram

If power corrupts,
does witch power corrupt absolutely?

A strange, inexplicable silence had settled down over the classroom. It was late in the afternoon, and the students no longer seemed restless—eager to escape to the freedom of the sweltering street. Instead, a thick lethargy had come upon them. It even extended to the teacher, who kept shaking her narrow head with its little black curls from side to side, as if to banish her languor by physical means, and with the quick petulance of a martyr to duty.

It was abnormally quiet, except for the monotone of one dispirited student reciting, and the crisp snap of the teacher's interruptions. Not even a whisper stirred the silence. The students were far too torpid to desire an exchange of confidences. Tinkling bells from an ice-cream cart jingled into the distance, and far away a lawn mower hummed meditatively.

Margaret basked near the open window, luxuriating in the golden feel of the sun on her bare arms and legs. She bent her head forward, so the genial rays would stroke the back of her neck, where the tawny hair was cut short and grew to a point.

Intense contentment swirled through her veins, beating rhythmically in the new blood that swelled her body. She wrote in her open notebook, carefully forming each letter: "Margaret. Margaret. Margaret."

And, because this bored her momentarily—although she would come back to it again and again—she reversed the letters. "Teragram. Teragram. Teragram."

She drew—not pictures but meaningless little designs which, she felt obscurely, had some meaning after all, a meaning that was just a little beyond her. Someday, as with all learning, she would understand. Meanwhile, she was young. She had time to wait.

All the time in the world.

There was one design in particular—a five-pointed star—that gave her great pleasure. It had to be drawn in a very special way, without lifting the pen from the paper. She drew several stars in this manner and experienced immense satisfaction.

A big iridescent fly, resplendently blue-green and

gold, buzzed inquisitively over the desk, attracted by the rich smell of the ink. She brushed it away.

"I am Margaret," she said to herself, thrilled with the secret knowledge of her own identity. "Yesterday I wasn't Margaret—at least, not the same Margaret. And tomorrow—who knows what I will be tomorrow?"

She gazed at the white skin of her arm admiringly. Once she'd been distressed because she could not tan, because her skin had retained a milky, almost storybook fairness, no matter how much she exposed herself to the sun. Now she realized that her whiteness was not only beautiful but right. It was the way she should be.

Already she seemed to feel her dress straining against her chest, and deep within her something seemed to whisper that, like chrysalis into butterfly, the change would be sudden, and immediate instead of gradual, as it was with human beings.

"I am becoming someone new and wonderful," she thought pleasurably. "I am Margaret. And I am thirteen."

And again she wrote "Margaret" and then "Teragram." Then, after a little thought, she added "Thirteen" . . . and the exciting five-pointed star with all the points connected by lines through the center.

"Margaret!"

The voice was not the delicious whispering of her

own mind. It came from outside, and was stern, peremptory, and brusque.

"Margaret!" the teacher repeated, more loudly. "Will you pay attention to me?"

Margaret lifted her eyes—large and green they were and a trifle protuberant—and stared at the teacher. "I'm sorry," she said, in a voice as soft and rich as clotted cream. But there was no real regret in it.

The teacher's voice sharpened antagonistically. "We were discussing Joan of Arc, Margaret. I asked what you could tell us about her."

Margaret's words were spaced sullenly apart from each other, as if dragging them out was an ordeal quite hateful to her. "She was a witch," she said. "The English burned her."

She lowered her head so that the warm sunlight would fall upon her neck again, and half closed her eyes, composing herself for a return to her ecstasy of contentment.

The teacher's thin lips curled. "They *said* she was a witch. But of course she wasn't a real witch. Well, Margaret? Was she? Answer me!"

Margaret raised her head. The movement coppered the top of her hair with sunlight, and set little flamelike reflections dancing in her eyes. She stared at the teacher through slitted lids.

"Of course she wasn't a real witch," she said, "or

they wouldn't have been able to burn her!"

Amusement rustled through the comatose class.

"Margaret!" The teacher rapped sharply with her pencil on the desk, although actually there had been no disturbance. "What nonsense is this?"

"But—no." The reply came even more slowly, as if the mouth and the vocal apparatus were Margaret's, but not the words themselves. "I was wrong. The witch lives on, but the body can be burned! So," Margaret concluded magnanimously, "Joan may have been a real witch, after all. But not a very good one."

The class laughed sleepily.

"Margaret!" The teacher's voice shook. So did the lower part of her face, where the flesh hung loose in spite of her thinness. It was not a pleasant sight and Margaret shut her eyes to avoid it.

"There are no such things as witches!" the teacher said, vehemently. "Joan of Arc was a blessed saint!"

"My great-great-great—I don't know how great, but *very* far back—grandmother was a witch," Margaret murmured, opening her eyes a little again. "The English burned her too, even though they were her own people. And she was no saint." The corners of her full pink lips quivered. "Truly, no one would ever call her a saint!"

The teacher's face pinched in disapproval. "I must speak to your mother about stuffing your head with stories like that!" she rasped. "Parents don't realize—"

With a sudden, startling gesture Margaret struck away the bluebottle fly that circled ardently about her head. "And she did not die either!" she declared angrily. "You can burn a witch. You can say that she does not exist. But neither will stop her from existing. She goes on and on, and there is nothing you or your kind can do to stop her!"

"Margaret, that will be enough!" the teacher shrilled. And, in an undertone, but not so low that the class could not catch the words, "Insolent! An intolerable child! I really will have to have a talk with her mother very soon."

Margaret lapsed into her torpor. Warm sunlight bathed her young body, and tiny rivulets of perspiration trickled down her temples and stung her eyes with warm saltiness. "Margaret," she wrote mechanically. "Teragram. Thirteen." And she drew several exciting stars, and other figures.

Oh, it was good to be Margaret, to be thirteen! Why it was so uniquely good, she could not be sure. Perhaps everyone felt that way upon becoming thirteen . . .

Perhaps it was only natural.

But this she did know: her mother had *not* told her about that other Margaret so far back in time. Way, way back it was—two, three, four, five hundred years.

A very long time. Her mother had said there was a legend that one of her remote ancestors had been a witch, but that was all. . . .

How had she known? And why had she wanted to strike the teacher dead for saying Joan of Arc was a saint?

Did it matter?

The sun's rays grew hotter, hotter, burning almost. She tried to move out of its range but it was almost as if she were bound hand and foot.

Bound . . .

The heat of the fire was growing agonizingly intense. The faggots around her feet were all ablaze now, and soon the flames would touch the beautiful white skin of which she had been so proud. They would burn her beautiful body too. Would she ever again get a body as smooth and as lovely? All that whiteness to char, to shrivel and turn black. Such a pity!

But there was no one to pity Margaret of Brentleigh except herself, nor were there any gods to whom she might pray. Her gods had no more power to help her than the breeze which blew smoke into her face.

It was a curious thing. The draft was chilly on her cheeks and forehead, and yet she was burning.

She could feel the heat of the approaching flames, but inside she was as cold as ice. Through the acrid smoke that rose thick in her nostrils she could still smell the dirt and the sweat and the dung and the perfume that pervaded the courtyard—all of the familiar odors she would never smell again on earth in that particular combination.

She tried to turn her face away, but she was too tightly bound to move even her head. The ropes bit deep into her flesh, but it would stay soft and white now for such a little time that the marring red weals were of no importance.

One of the bowmen laughed at her coughing. Others began circling about the fire, their white teeth and the bright arrows they wore under their belts glinting in the light of the flames. It wasn't every day that they could enjoy the spectacle of a young and beautiful witch being burned, her body so starkly naked that they could watch every quiver as it slowly charred.

It was known to everyone who watched that the cries of a witch burning were celestial music to give pleasure to God-fearing folk.

Only she would *not* scream. She'd be damned if she'd give them that satisfaction—and she laughed a little at her blasphemous choice of words.

Beyond the bowmen, motionless on his black stallion, his face as rigid as one of the statues in the ca-

thedral his family's gold had helped to build . . . sat
John Aleyn. The somber cloak in which he was wrapped
hid the raven-dark, curly hair on which she had so
doted, and in the leaping light of the fire his carven
face seemed almost that of an old man.

Yet he was but one-and-twenty—scarcely five years
her senior.

It had been said that should a witch love truly, her
undoing would follow as quickly as the cooling of her
paramour's ardor and so it had turned out, as she had
known it would. But did he think that by burning her
body he could save his soul? The stupid, cowardly fool!
He was wrong, wrong—his soul was already pledged
to eternal fire!

She opened her flame-red mouth and laughed, so
defiantly and scornfully that even the bowmen were
taken aback. Some crossed themselves and she thought
she saw a momentary change of expression on Aleyn's
face, a flicker in his glass-gray eyes. But it might only
have been the leaping of the firelight.

"What ails you, wench?" asked the nearest bowman,
a man who often in her infancy had dandled her on his
knee, and who now made as if he did not even know
her. "Do you mock the fire that will consume you now
and forever?"

"Do you think you can kill a witch with a little
fire?" she demanded in her turn, her eyes blazing with
fury.

"Fire has killed witches before," he said sullenly. "It will kill you as well."

"The body, yes! But never the rest of me. Watch yourselves! You, Jenkin, and you—and you! Watch yourselves and your wives, and your children. Even your cattle will not be safe, for my curse is upon you, now and forever."

The bowman stepped back in horror, his cheeks pallid in the firelight. "I' Faith, my lord," he said to Aleyn, "there's no man readier than I to do the Church's bidding. But I love my good wife and my little ones well, and I would not—"

"Pay the witch no heed," he nobleman said, his face still impassive.

Yet once he had loved her. It was of his own will that he'd slept in her arms, and she had been a maid the first time and he the only man who ever had touched her. Ay, and the only *being* who had ever touched her, despite what the folk said. But they had turned him against her, and he had betrayed her, as she had known he would. One of the penalties of being a witch was that you could take but little pleasure in the present, knowing all too well what the future would bring.

He had betrayed her to save his own skin, had turned upon her so that he would not also be accused and burn with her. And watching from the tower window, mocking her torment and despair, was brown Allison, the

Abbot's ugly niece who was to wed Aleyn at Whit-suntide. To wed Aleyn for all eternity.

But Aleyn would find the wedding worse than the burning he'd escaped. Had there been another man of gentle birth willing to espouse the ardent, black-tressed toad, he might have joined Margaret at the stake, for all of his betrayals and protestations. And the Abbot would have made good use of the gold and broad acres that would have fallen forfeit to the Church.

"Pay the witch no heed," Aleyn repeated. "When a witch burns, she dies, and her soul goes to everlasting torment." He crossed himself. "So the Church has said."

"A witch never dies!" Margaret declared, her voice firm through the pain that was beginning to sear her body. "I shall live again and again. I have a daughter, as you know—your own blood as well as mine. She has been hid away where you will never find her for all of your searching, and she will be a witch. Yes, and of her children, another shall be a witch, and in each succeeding generation still another, as she grows to womanhood, shall bear my image. Not from mother to daughter will the heritage pass, but from a chosen one to the next who is best fitted to be sorcery's hand-maiden. Thus will my spirit pass down through the ages, gaining strength with each century. How does it feel to sire a line of witches, my Lord? Does it not please you well?"

The young man's old face was still, save for the movement of his lips as he ordered: "Throw more faggots on the fire."

The flames leaped high, becoming a burning, tearing agony in the body that was, regrettably, human. Fire . . . heat . . . pain . . .

Margaret screamed.

"Margaret!" The teacher, alarmed, half rose from her chair. "What's the matter, child?"

Margaret rubbed her eyes, and looked up dazedly. "It's nothing. I'm sorry. The sun was so hot it—it made me feel dizzy."

The class giggled with amusement, and relief.

The teacher sank back in her seat. "No wonder! You should have had more sense than to let it beat right down on you like that. You might have gotten a sunstroke. Will one of you boys draw the blind?"

One of the students obeyed.

Now Margaret's face was obscured by shadow. But the shadow was a warm caressing obscurity, and the face half lost in it was still Margaret's. She was Margaret and something more. She had known it was something more when the strange, the new, the almost frightening sensation had first come to her. Only it was no longer frightening. Now she knew she would be a witch when she became a woman. But—when would she become a woman?

Margaret of Brentleigh had died at sixteen, already a mother. Girls had become women early in those days. Probably *that* Margaret would have considered a thirteen-year-old girl a woman grown.

The newest Margaret gazed with pleasure at her curving forearm and the slender, milk-pale fingers that wrote "Margaret, Margaret, Teragram, Teragram . . ." and went on to draw stars and other signs and figures less comprehensible to her conscious mind, but not—she realized now—mere doodlings.

"Almost as if they didn't belong to me," she thought, watching the diligent fingers. "But still I can control them. I can control . . . control . . ."

The ubiquitous bluebottle fly whirred around her face again, buzzing amorously.

"Pest!" she shrieked, but quietly, inside of her mind, for she was still, not exactly afraid, but a little hesitant of the teacher. "I wish you were dead!"

The insect fell to the desk and lay there . . . stiff, unmoving.

She prodded the little body with her pen. It was dead all right.

Dead. She was a witch. A full-fledged witch! Power and control . . . hers. She spread her slender hands wide to grasp an almost tangible ecstasy from the air.

"Margaret!" the teacher's voice came—sharp, hostile. "Margaret, you're not paying attention again!"

The voice was ugly; the teacher was ugly—and old. Both should not be permitted to exist. For Margaret loved pretty things. Young things.

Margaret opened her heavy-lidded green eyes wide and looked speculatively at the teacher. . . .

Zenna Henderson

Stevie and The Dark

*Sometimes there's nothing better
than the magic of a child.*

The Dark lived in a hole in the bank of the sand wash
where Stevie liked to play. The Dark wanted to come
out, but Stevie had fixed it so it couldn't. He put a
row of special little magic rocks in front of the hole.
Stevie knew they were magic because he found them
himself and they felt like magic. When you are as old
as Stevie—five—a whole hand of years old—you know
lots of things and you know what magic feels like.

Stevie had the rocks in his pockets when he first
found The Dark. He had been digging a garage in the
side of the wash when a piece of the bank came loose
and slid down onto him. One rock hit him on the forehead hard enough to make him cry—if he had been
only four. But Stevie was five, so he wiped the blood
with the back of his hand and scraped away the dirt

to find the big spoon Mommy let him take to dig with. Then he saw that the hole was great big and his spoon was just inside it. So he reached in for it and The Dark came out a little ways and touched Stevie. It covered up his hand clear to the wrist and when Stevie jerked away, his hand was cold and all skinned across the back. For a minute it was white and stiff, then the blood came out and it hurt and Stevie got mad. So he took out the magic rocks and put the little red one down in front of the hole. The Dark came out again with just a little finger-piece and touched the red rock, but it didn't like the magic so it started to push around it. Stevie put down the other little rocks—the round smooth white ones and the smooth yellow ones.

The Dark made a lot of little fingers that were trying to get past the magic. There was just one hole left, so Stevie put down the black see-through rock he found that morning. Then The Dark pulled back all the little fingers and began to pour over the black rock. So, quick like a rabbit, Stevie drew a magic in the sand and The Dark pulled back into the hole again. Then Stevie marked King's X all around the hole and ran to get some more magic rocks. He found a white one with a band of blue around the middle and another yellow one. He went back and put the rocks in front of the hole and rubbed out the King's X. The Dark got mad and piled up behind the rocks until it was higher than Stevie's head.

Stevie was scared, but he stood still and held tight to his pocket piece. He knew that was the magicest of all. Juanito had told him so and Juanito knew. He was ten years old and the one who told Stevie about magic in the first place. He had helped Stevie make the magic. He was the one who did the writing on the pocket piece. Of course, Stevie would know how to write after he went to school, but that was a long time away.

The Dark couldn't ever hurt him while he held the magic, but it was kind of scary to see The Dark standing up like that in the bright hot sunshine. The Dark didn't have any head or arms or legs or body. It didn't have any eyes either, but it was looking at Stevie. It didn't have any mouth, but it was mumbling at Stevie. He could hear it inside his head and the mumbles were hate, so Stevie squatted down in the sand and drew a magic again—a big magic—and The Dark jerked back into the hole. Stevie turned and ran as fast as he could until the mumbles in his ears turned into fast wind and the sound of rattling rocks on the road.

Next day Arnold came with his mother to visit at Stevie's house. Stevie didn't like Arnold. He was a tattletale and a crybaby even if he was a whole hand and two more fingers old. Stevie took him down to the sand wash to play. They didn't go down where The Dark was, but while they were digging tunnels around the roots of the cottonwood tree, Stevie could feel The

Dark, like a long deep thunder that only your bones could hear—not your ears. He knew the big magic he wrote in the sand was gone and The Dark was trying to get past the magic rocks.

Pretty soon Arnold began to brag.

"I got a space gun."

Stevie threw some more sand backward. "So've I," he said.

"I got a two-wheel bike."

Stevie sat back on his heels. "Honest?"

"Sure!" Arnold talked real smarty. "You're too little to have a two-wheel bike. You couldn't ride it if you had one."

"Could too." Stevie went back to his digging, feeling bad inside. He had fallen off Rusty's bike when he tried to ride it. Arnold didn't know it though.

"Could not." Arnold caved in his tunnel. "I've got a BB gun and a real saw and a cat with three-and-a-half legs."

Stevie sat down in the sand. What could you get better than a cat with three-and-a-half legs? He traced a magic in the sand.

"I've got something you haven't."

"Have not." Arnold caved in Stevie's tunnel.

"Have too. It's a Dark."

"A what?"

"A Dark. I've got it in a hole down there." He jerked his head down the wash.

"Aw, you're crazy. There ain't no dark. You're just talking baby stuff."

Stevie felt his face getting hot. "I am not. You just come and see."

He dragged Arnold by the hand down the wash with the sand crunching under foot like spilled sugar and sifting in and out of their barefoot sandals. They squatted in front of the hole. The Dark had pulled way back in so they couldn't see it.

"I don't see nothing." Arnold leaned forward to look into the hole. "There ain't no dark. You're just silly."

"I am not! And The Dark is so in that hole."

"Sure it's dark in the hole, but that ain't nothing. You can't have a dark, silly."

"Can too." Stevie reached in his pocket and took tight hold of his pocket piece. "You better cross your fingers. I'm going to let it out a little ways."

"Aw!" Arnold didn't believe him, but he crossed his fingers anyway.

Stevie took two of the magic rocks away from in front of the hole and moved back. The Dark came pouring out like a flood. It poured in a thin stream through the open place in the magic and shot up like a tower of smoke. Arnold was so surprised that he uncrossed his fingers and The Dark wrapped around his head and he began to scream and scream. The Dark sent a long arm out to Stevie, but Stevie pulled out

his pocket piece and hit The Dark. Stevie could hear
The Dark scream inside his head so he hit it again and
The Dark fell all together and got littler so Stevie
pushed it back into the hole with his pocket piece. He
put the magic rocks back and wrote two big magics in
the sand so that The Dark cried again and hid way
back in the hole.

Arnold was lying on the sand with his face all white
and stiff, so Stevie shook him and called him. Arnold
opened his eyes and his face turned red and began to
bleed. He started to bawl, "Mama! Mama!" and ran
for the house as fast as he could through the soft sand.
Stevie followed him, yelling, "You uncrossed your fingers! It's your fault! You uncrossed your fingers!"

Arnold and his mother went home. Arnold was still
bawling and his mother was real red around the nose
when she yelled at Mommy. "You'd better learn to
control that brat of yours or he'll grow up a murderer!
Look what he did to my poor Arnold!" And she drove
away so fast that she hit the chuckhole by the gate
and nearly went off the road.

Mommy sat down on the front step and took Stevie
between her knees. Stevie looked down and traced a
little, soft magic with his finger on Mommy's slacks.

"What happened, Stevie?"

Stevie squirmed. "Nothing, Mommy. We were just
playing in the wash."

"Why did you hurt Arnold?"

"I didn't. Honest. I didn't even touch him."

"But the whole side of his face was skinned." Mommy put on her no-fooling-now voice. "Tell me what happened, Stevie."

Stevie gulped. "Well, Arnold was bragging 'bout his two-wheel bike and—" Stevie got excited and looked up. "And Mommy, he has a cat with three-and-a-half legs!"

"Go on."

Stevie leaned against her again.

"Well, I've got a Dark in a hole in the wash so I—"

"A Dark? What is that?"

"It's, it's just a Dark. It isn't very nice. I keep it in its hole with magic. I let it out a little bit to show Arnold and it hurt him. But it was his fault. He uncrossed his fingers."

Mommy sighed. "What *really* happened, Stevie?"

"I told you, Mommy! Honest, that's what happened."

"For True, Stevie?" She looked right in his eyes.

Stevie looked right back. "Yes, Mommy, For True."

She sighed again. "Well, son, I guess this Dark business is the same as your Mr. Bop and Toody Troot."

"Uh, uh!" Stevie shook his head. "No sir. Mr. Bop and Toody Troot are nice. The Dark is bad."

"Well, don't play with it anymore then."

"I *don't* play with it," protested Stevie. "I just keep it shut up with magic."

"All right, son." She stood up and brushed the dust off the back of her slacks. "Only for the love of Toody Troot, don't let Arnold get hurt again." She smiled at Stevie.

Stevie smiled back. "Okay, Mommy. But it was his fault. He uncrossed his fingers. He's a baby."

The next time Stevie was in the wash playing cowboy on Burro Eddie, he heard The Dark calling him. It called so sweet and soft that anybody would think it was something nice, but Stevie could feel the bad rumble way down under the nice, so he made sure his pocket piece was handy, shooed Eddie away, and went down to the hole and squatted down in front of it.

The Dark stood up behind the magic rocks and it had made itself look like Arnold only its eyes didn't match and it had forgotten one ear and it was freckled all over like Arnold's face.

"Hello," said The Dark with its Arnold-mouth. "Let's play."

"No," said Stevie. "You can't fool me. You're still The Dark."

"I won't hurt you." The Arnold-face stretched out sideways to make a smile, but it wasn't a very good one. "Let me out and I'll show you how to have lots of fun."

"No," said Stevie. "If you weren't bad, the magic couldn't hold you. I don't want to play with bad things."

"Why not?" asked The Dark. "Being bad is fun sometimes—lots of fun."

"I guess it is," said Stevie, "but only if it's a little bad. A big bad makes your stomach sick and you have to have a spanking or a sit-in-the-corner and then a big loving from Mommy or Daddy before it gets well again."

"Aw, come on," said The Dark. "I'm lonesome. Nobody ever comes to play with me. I like you. Let me out and I'll give you a two-wheel bike."

"Really?" Stevie felt all warm inside. "For True?"

"For True. And a cat with three-and-a-half legs."

"Oh!" Stevie felt like Christmas morning. "Honest?"

"Honest. All you have to do is take away the rocks and break up your pocket piece and I'll fix everything for you."

"My pocket piece?" The warmness was going away. "No sir, I won't either break it up. It's the magicest thing I've got and it was hard to make."

"But I can give you some better magic."

"Nothing can be more magic." Stevie tightened his hand around his pocket piece. "Anyway, Daddy said I might get a two-wheel bike for my birthday. I'll be six years old. How old are you?"

The Dark moved back and forth. "I'm as old as the world."

Stevie laughed. "Then you must know Auntie Phronie. Daddy says she's as old as the hills."

"The hills are young," said The Dark. "Come on, Stevie, let me out. Please—pretty please."

"Well." Stevie reached for the pretty red rock. "Promise you'll be good."

"I promise."

Stevie hesitated. He could feel a funniness in The Dark's voice. It sounded like Lili-cat when she purred to the mice she caught. It sounded like Pooch-pup when he growled softly to the gophers he ate sometimes. It made Stevie feel funny inside and, as he squatted there wondering what the feeling was, lightning flashed brightly above the treetops and a few big raindrops splashed down with the crash of thunder.

"Well," said Stevie, standing up, feeling relieved. "It's going to rain. I can't play with you now. I have to go. Maybe I can come see you tomorrow."

"No, now!" said The Dark. "Let me out right now!" and its Arnold-face was all twisted and one eye was slipping down one cheek.

Stevie started to back away, his eyes feeling big and scared. "Another time. I can't play in the wash when it storms. There might be a flood."

"Let me out!" The Dark was getting madder. The Arnold-face turned purple and its eyes ran down its face like sick fire and it melted back into blackness again. "Let me out!" The Dark hit the magic so hard that it shook the sand and one of the rocks started to roll. Quick like a rabbit, Stevie pressed the rock down hard and fixed all the others too. Then The Dark twisted itself into a thing so awful-looking that Stevie's stomach got sick and he wanted to upchuck. He took out his pocket piece and drew three hard magics in the sand and The Dark screamed so hard that Stevie screamed, too, and ran home to Mommy and was very sick.

Mommy put him to bed and gave him some medicine to comfort his stomach and told Daddy he'd better buy Stevie a hat. The sun was too hot for a towheaded, bareheaded boy in the middle of July.

Stevie stayed away from the wash for a while after that, but one day Burro Eddie opened the gate with his teeth again and wandered off down the road, headed for the wash. It had been storming again in the Whetstones. Mommy said, "You'd better go after Eddie. The flood will be coming down the wash this afternoon and if Eddie gets caught, he'll get washed right down into the river."

"Aw, Eddie can swim," said Stevie.

"Sure he can, but not in a flash flood. Remember what happened to Durkin's horse last year."

"Yeah," said Stevie, wide-eyed. "It got drownded.

It even went over the dam. It was dead."

"Very dead," laughed Mommy. "So you scoot along and bring Eddie back. But remember, if there's any water at all in the wash, you stay out of it. And if any water starts down while you're in it, get out in a hurry."

"Okay, Mommy."

So Stevie put on his sandals—there were too many stickers on the road to go barefoot—and went after Eddie. He tracked him carefully like Daddy showed him—all bent over—and only had to look twice to see where he was so he'd be sure to follow the right tracks. He finally tracked him down into the wash.

Burro Eddie was eating mesquite beans off a bush across the wash from The Dark. Stevie held out his hand and waggled his fingers at him.

"Come on, Eddie. Come on, old feller."

Eddie waggled his ears at Stevie and peeked out of the corner of his eyes, but he went on pulling at the long beans, sticking his teeth way out so the thorns wouldn't scratch his lips so bad. Stevie walked slow and careful toward Eddie, making soft talk real coaxing-like and was just sliding his hand up Eddie's shoulder to get hold of the ragged old rope around his neck when Eddie decided to be scared and jumped with all four feet. He skittered across to the other side of the wash, tumbling Stevie down on the rough, gravelly sand.

"Daggone you, Eddie!" he yelled, getting up. "You

come on back here. We gotta get out of the wash.
Mommy's gonna be mad at us. Don't be so mean!"

Stevie started after Eddie and Eddie kept on playing
like he was scared. He flapped his stringy tail and tried
to climb the almost straight-up-and-down bank of the
wash. His front feet scrabbled at the bank and his hind
feet kicked up the sand. Then he slid down on all fours
and just stood there, his head pushed right up against
the bank, not moving at all.

Stevie walked up to him real slow and started to
take the old rope. Then he saw where Eddie was standing.

"Aw, Eddie," he said, squatting down in the sand.
Look what you went and did. You kicked all my magic
away. You let The Dark get out. Now I haven't got
anything Arnold hasn't got. Dern you, Eddie!" He
stood up and smacked Eddie's flank with one hand.
But Eddie just stood there and his flank felt funny—
kinda stiff and cold.

"Eddie!" Stevie dragged on the rope and Eddie's
head turned—jerky—like an old gate. Then Eddie's
feet moved, but slow and funny, until Eddie turned
around.

"What's the matter, Eddie?" Stevie put his hand on
Eddie's nose and looked at him close. Something was
wrong with the burro's eyes. They were still big and
dark, but now they didn't seem to see Stevie or anything—they looked empty. And while Stevie looked

into them, there came a curling blackness into them,
like smoke coming through a crack and all at once the
eyes began to see again. Stevie started to back away,
his hands going out in front of him.

"Eddie," he whispered. "Eddie, what's the matter?"
And Eddie started after him—but not like Eddie—
not with fast feet that kicked the sand in little spurts,
but slow and awful, the two legs on one side together,
then the two legs on the other side—like a sawhorse
or something that wasn't used to four legs. Stevie's
heart began to pound under his T-shirt and he backed
away faster. "Eddie, Eddie," he pleaded. "Don't, Eddie.
Don't act like that. Be good. We gotta go back to the
house."

But Eddie kept on coming, faster and faster, his
legs getting looser so they worked better and his eyes
staring at Stevie. Stevie backed away until he ran into
a big old cottonwood trunk that high water brought
down after the last storm. He ducked around in back
of the trunk. Eddie just kept on dragging his feet
through the sand until he ran into the trunk too, but
his feet kept on moving, even when he couldn't go any
farther. Stevie put out one shaky hand to pat Eddie's
nose. But he jerked it back and stared and stared
across the tree trunk at Eddie. And Eddie stared back
with eyes that were wide and shiny like quiet lightning. Stevie swallowed dryness in his throat and then
he knew.

"The Dark!" he whispered. "The Dark. It got out. It got in Eddie!"

He turned and started to run kitty-cornered across the wash. There was an awful scream from Eddie. Not a donkey scream at all, and Stevie looked back and saw Eddie—The Dark—coming after him, only his legs were working better now and his big mouth was wide open with the big yellow teeth all wet and shiny. The sand was sucking at Stevie's feet, making him stumble. He tripped over something and fell. He scrambled up again and his hands splashed as he scrambled. The runoff from the Whetstones was coming and Stevie was in the wash!

He could hear Eddie splashing behind him. Stevie looked back and screamed and ran for the bank. Eddie's face wasn't Eddie anymore. Eddie's mouth looked full of twisting darkness and Eddie's legs had learned how a donkey runs and Eddie could outrun Stevie any day of the week. The water was coming higher and he could feel it grab his feet and suck sand out from under him every step he took.

Somewhere far away he heard Mommy shrieking at him, "Stevie! Get out of the wash!"

Then Stevie was scrambling up the steep bank, the stickers getting in his hands and the fine silty dirt getting in his eyes. He could hear Eddie coming and he heard Mommy screaming, "Eddie!" and there was

Eddie trying to come up the bank after him, his mouth wide and slobbering.

Then Stevie got mad. "Dern you, old Dark!" he screamed. "You leave Eddie alone!" He was hanging on to the bushes with one hand but he dug into his pocket with the other and pulled out his pocket piece. He looked down at it—his precious pocket piece—two pieces of Popsicle stick tied together so they looked a little bit like an airplane, and on the top, lopsided and scraggly, the magic letters INRI. Stevie squeezed it tight, and then he screamed and threw it right down Eddie's throat—right into the swirling nasty blackness inside of Eddie.

There was an awful scream from Eddie and a big bursting roar and Stevie lost hold of the bush and fell down into the racing, roaring water. Then Mommy was there gathering him up, crying his name over and over as she waded to a low place in the bank, the water curling above her knees, making her stagger. Stevie hung on tight and cried, "Eddie! Eddie! That mean old Dark! He made me throw my pocket piece away! Oh, Mommy, Mommy! Where's Eddie?"

And he and Mommy cried together in the stickery sand up on the bank of the wash while the flood waters roared and rumbled down to the river, carrying Eddie away, sweeping the wash clean, from bank to bank.

William M. Lee

A Message from Charity

This is a story of a timeless love.

That summer of the year 1700 was the hottest in the memory of the very oldest inhabitants. Because the year ushered in a new century, some held that the events were related and that for a whole hundred years Bay Colony would be as torrid and steamy as the Indies themselves.

There was a good deal of illness in Annes Towne, and a score had died before the weather broke at last in late September. For the great part they were oldsters who succumbed, but some of the young were sick too, and Charity Paynes as sick as any.

Charity had turned eleven in the spring and had still the figure and many of the ways of thinking of a child, but she was tall and strong and tanned by the New England sun, for she spent many hours helping her

father in the fields and trying to keep some sort of
order in the dooryard and garden.

During the weeks when she lay bedridden and, for
a time, burning up with the fever, Thomas Carter and
his good wife Beulah came as neighbors should to lend
a hand, for Charity's mother had died abirthing and
Obie Payne could not cope all alone.

Charity lay on a pallet covered by a straw-filled
mattress which her father, frantic to be doing something for her and finding little enough to do beyond
the saying of short fervent prayers, refilled with fresh
straw as often as Beulah would allow. A few miles
down Harmon Brook was a famous beaver pond where
in winter the Annes Towne people cut ice to be stored
under layers of bark and chips. It had been used heavily early in the summer, and there was not very much
ice left, but those families with sickness in the home
might draw upon it for the patient's comfort. So Charity had bits of ice folded into a woolen cloth to lay on
her forehead when the fever was bad.

William Trowbridge, who had apprenticed in medicine down in Philadelphia, attended the girl, and pronounced her illness a sort of summer cholera which
was claiming victims all up and down the brook. Trowbridge was only moderately esteemed in Annes Towne,
being better, it was said, at delivering lambs and foals
than at treating human maladies. He was a gruff and
notional man, and he was prone to state his views on

a subject and then walk away instead of waiting to argue and perhaps be refuted. Not easy to get along with.

For Charity he prescribed a diet of beef tea with barley and another tea, very unpleasant to the taste, made from pounded willow bark. What was more, all her drinking water was to be boiled. Since there was no other advice to be had, they followed it and in due course Charity got well.

She ran a great fever for five days, and it was midway in this period when the strange dreams began. Not dreams really, for she was awake though often out of her senses, knowing her father now and then, other times seeing him as a gaunt and frightening stranger. When she was better, still weak but wholly rational, she tried to tell her visitors about these dreams.

"Some person was talking and talking," she recalled. "A man or perchance a lad. He talked not to me, but I could hear or understand all that he said. 'Twas strange talk indeed, a porridge of the King's English and other words of no sense at all. And with the talk I did see some fearful sights."

"La, now, don't even think of it," said Dame Beulah.

"But I would fain both think and talk of it, for I am no longer afeared. Such things I saw in bits and flashes, as 'twere seen by a strike of lightning."

"Talk an ye be so minded, then. There's naught impious in y'r conceits. Tell me again about the carriages which traveled along with nary horse."

Annes Towne survived the Revolution and the War of 1812, and for a time seemed likely to become a larger, if not an important community. But when its farms became less productive and the last virgin timber disappeared from the area, Annes Towne began to disappear too, dwindling from two score of homes to a handful, then to none; and the last foundation had crumbled to rubble and been scattered a hundred years before it could have been nominated a historic site.

In time dirt tracks became stone roads, which gave way to black meanderings of macadam, and these in their turn were displaced by never ending bands of concrete. The cross-roads site of Annes Towne was presently cleared of brambles, sumac and red cedar, and overnight it was a shopping center. Now, for mile on spreading mile the New England hills were dotted with ranch houses, salt boxes and split-level colonial homes.

During four decades Harmon Brook had been fouled and poisoned by a textile bleach and dye works. Rising labor costs had at last driven the small company to extinction. With that event and increasingly rigorous legislation, the stream had come back to the extent that it could now be bordered by some of these prosperous homes and by the golf course of the Anniston Country Club.

With aquatic plants and bullfrogs and a few fish

inhabiting its waters, it was not obvious to implicate the Harmon for the small outbreak of typhoid which occurred in the hot dry summer of 1965. No one was dependent on it for drinking water. To the discomfort of a local milk distributor, who was entirely blameless, indictment of the stream was delayed and obscured by the fact that the organisms involved were not a typical strain of *Salmonella typhosa*. Indeed they ultimately found a place in the American Type Culture Collection, under a new number.

Young Peter Wood, whose home was one of those pleasantly situated along the stream, was the most seriously ill of all the cases, partly because he was the first, mostly because his symptoms went unremarked for a time. Peter was sixteen and not highly communicative to either parents or friends. The Woods Senior both taught, at Harvard and Wellesley respectively. They were intelligent and well-intentioned parents, but sometimes a little off-hand, and like many of their friends, they raised their son to be a miniature adult in as many ways as possible. His sports, tennis and golf, were adult sports. His reading tastes were catholic, ranging from Camus to Al Capp to science fiction. He had been carefully held back in his progress through the lower grades so that he would not enter college more than a year or so ahead of his age. He had an adequate number of friends and sufficient areas of congeniality with them. He had gotten a driver's license shortly after his sixteenth birthday and drove seriously and well enough to be allowed nearly unrestricted use of the second car.

So Peter Wood was not the sort of boy to complain to his family about headache, mild nausea and other symptoms. Instead, after they had persisted for forty-eight hours, he telephoned for an appointment on his own initiative and visited their family doctor. Suddenly, in the waiting room, he became much worse, and was given a cot in an examining room until Dr. Maxwell was free to drive him home. The doctor did not seriously suspect typhoid, though it was among several possibilities which he counted as less likely.

Peter's temperature rose from 104° to over 105° that night. No nurse was to be had until morning, and his parents alternated in attendance in his bedroom. There was no cause for alarm, since the patient was full of wide-spectrum antibiotic. But he slept only fitfully with intervals of waking delirium. He slapped at the sheet, tossed around on the bed and muttered or spoke now and then. Some of the talk was understandable.

"There's a forest," he said.

"What?" asked his father.

"There's a forest the other side of the stream."

"Oh."

"Can you see it?"

"No, I'm sitting inside here with you. Take it easy, son."

"Some deer are coming down to drink, along the edge of Weller's pasture."

"Is that so?"

"Last year a mountain lion killed two of them, right where they drank. Is it raining?"

"No, it isn't. It would be fine if we could have some."

"It's raining. I can hear it on the roof." A pause. "It drips down the chimney."

Peter turned his head to look at his father, momentarily clear eyed.

"How long since there's been a forest across the stream?"

Dr. Wood reflected on the usual difficulty of answering explicit questions and on his own ignorance of history.

"A long time. I expect this valley has been farm land since colonial days."

"Funny," Peter said. "I shut my eyes and I can see a forest. Really big trees. On our side of the stream there's a kind of garden and an apple tree and a path goes down to the water."

"It sounds pleasant."

"Yeah."

"Why don't you try going to sleep?"

"OK."

The antibiotic accomplished much less than it should have done in Peter's case, and he stayed very sick for several days. Even after diagnosis, there appeared no good reason to move him from home. A trained nurse was on duty after that first night, and tranquilizers and sedatives reduced her job to no more than keeping a watch. There were only a few sleepy communications from her young patient. It was on the fourth night, the last one when he had any significant fever, that he asked:

"Were you ever a girl?"

"Well, thanks a lot. I'm not as old as all that."

"I mean, were you ever inside a girl?"

"I think you'd better go back to sleep, young man."

"I mean—I guess I don't know what I mean."

He uttered no oddities thereafter, at least when there was anyone within hearing. During the days of his recovery and convalescence, abed and later stretched out on a chaise longue on the terrace looking down toward Harmon Brook, he took to whispering. He moved his lips hardly at all, but vocalized each word, or if he fell short of this, at least put each thought into carefully chosen words and sentences.

The idea that he might be in mental communication with another person was not, to him, very startling. Steeped in the lore of science fiction whose heroes were, as like as not, adepts at telepathy, the event seemed almost an expected outcome of his wishes. Many nights he had lain awake sending out (he hoped) a mental probe, trying and trying to find the trick, for surely there must be one, of making a contact.

Now that such a contact was established he sought, just as vainly, for some means to prove it. How do you know you're not dreaming, he asked himself. How do you know you're not still delirious?

The difficulty was that his communication with Charity Payne could be by mental route only. Had there been any possibility for Peter to reach the girl by mail, by telephone, by travel and a personal visit, their rapport on a mental level might have been confirmed, and their messages cross-checked.

During their respective periods of illness, Peter and Charity achieved a communion of a sort which consisted at first of brief glimpses, each of the other's environment. They were not—then—seeing through one another's eyes so much as tapping one another's visual recollections. While Peter stared at a smoothly plastered ceiling, Charity looked at rough-hewn beams. He, when his aching head permitted, could turn on one side and watch a television program. She, by the same movement, could see a small smoky fire in a monstrous stone fireplace, where water was heated and her beef and barley broth kept steaming.

Instead of these current images, current for each of them in their different times, they saw stored-up pictures, not perfect, for neither of them was remembering perfectly; rather like pictures viewed through a badly ground lens, with only the objects of principal interest in clear detail.

Charity saw her fearful sights with no basis for comprehension—a section of dual highway animated by hurtling cars and trucks and not a person, recognizable as a person, in sight; a tennis court, and what on earth could it be; a jet plane crossing the sky; a vast and many storied building which glinted with glass and the silvery tracings of untarnished steel.

At the start she was terrified nearly out of her wits. It's all very well to dream, and a nightmare is only a bad dream after you waken, but a nightmare is assembled from familiar props. You could reasonably be chased by a dragon (like the one in the picture that St. George had to fight) or be lost in a cave (like the one on Parish Hill, only bigger and darker). To dream of things which have no meaning at all is worse.

She was spared prolongation of her terror by Peter's comprehension of their situation and his intuitive realization of what the experience, assuming a two-way channel, might be doing to her. The vignettes of her life which he was seeing were in no way disturbing. Everything he saw through her mind was within his framework of reference. Horses and cattle, fields and forest, rutted lanes and narrow wooden bridges, were things he knew, even if he did not live among them. He recognized Harmon Brook because, directly below their home, there was an immense granite boulder parting the flow, shaped like a great bear-like animal with its head down, drinking. It was strange that the stream, in all those years, had neither silted up nor eroded away to hide or change the seeming of the rock, but so it was. He saw it through Charity's eyes and knew the place in spite of the forest on the far hill.

When he first saw this partly familiar, partly strange scene, he heard from somewhere within his mind the frightened cry of a little girl. His thinking at that time was fever distorted and incoherent. It was two days later after a period of several hours of normal temperature, when he conceived the idea—with sudden virtual certainty—these pastoral scenes he had been dreaming were truly something seen with other eyes. There were subtle perceptual differences between those pictures and his own seeing.

To his mother, writing at a table near the windows, he said, "I think I'm feeling better. How about a glass of orange juice?"

She considered. "The doctor should be here in an hour or so. In the meantime you can make do with a little more ice water. I'll get it. Drink it slowly, remember."

Two hundred and sixty-five years away, Charity Payne thought suddenly, "How about a glass of orange juice?" She had been drowsing, but her eyes popped wide open. "Mercy," she said aloud. Dame Beulah bent over the pallet.

"What is it, child?"

"How about a glass of orange juice?" Charity repeated.

"La, 'tis gibberish." A cool hand was laid on her forehead. "Would ye like a bit of ice to bite on?"

Orange juice, whatever that might be, was forgotten.

Over the next several days Peter Wood tried time and again to address the stranger directly, and repeatedly failed. Some of what he said to others reached her in fragments and further confused her state of mind. What she had to say, on the other hand, was coming through to him with increasing frequency. Often it was only a word or a phrase with a quaint twist like a historical novel, and he would lie puzzling over it, trying to place the person on the other end of their erratic line of communication. His recognition of Bear Rock, which he had seen once again through her eyes, was disturbing. His science fiction conditioning led him naturally to speculate about the parallel worlds concept, but that seemed not to fit the facts as he saw them.

Peter reached the stage of convalescence when he could spend all day on the terrace and look down, when he wished, at the actual rock. There, for the hundredth time he formed the syllables "Hello, who are you?" and for the first time received a response. It was a silence, but a silence reverberating with shock, totally different in quality from the blankness which had met him before.

"My name is Peter Wood."

There was a long pause before the answer came, softly and timidly.

"My name is Charity Payne. Where are you? What is happening to me?"

The following days of enforced physical idleness were filled with exploration and discovery. Peter found out almost at once that, while they were probably no more than a few feet apart in their respective worlds, a gulf of more than a quarter of a thousand years stretched between them. Such a contact through time was a greater departure from known physical laws, certainly, than the mere fact of telepathic communication. Peter reveled in his growing ability.

In another way the situation was heartbreaking: No matter how well they came to know one another, he realized, they could never meet, and after no more than a few hours of acquaintance he found that he was regarding this naive child of another time with esteem and a sort of affection.

They arrived shortly at a set of rules which seemed to govern and limit their communications. Each came to be able to hear the other speak, whether aloud or subvocally. Each learned to perceive through the other's senses, up to a point. Visual perception became better and better especially for direct seeing while, as they grew more skillful, the remembered scene became less clear. Tastes and odors could be transmitted, if not accurately, at least with the expected response. Tactile sensations could not be perceived in the slightest degree.

There was little that Peter Wood could learn from Charity. He came to recognize her immediate associates and liked them, particularly her gaunt, weatherbeaten father. He formed a picture of Puritanism which, as an ethic, he had to respect, while the supporting dogma evoked nothing but impatience. At first he exposed her to the somewhat scholarly agnosticism which prevailed in his own home, but soon found that it distressed her deeply and he left off. There was so much he could report from the vantage of 1965, so many things he could show her which did not conflict with her tenets and faith.

He discovered that Charity's ability to read was remarkable, though what she had read was naturally limited—the Bible from cover to cover, *Pilgrim's Progress*, several essays and two of Shakespeare's plays. Encouraged by a schoolmaster who must have been an able and dedicated man, she had read and reread everything permitted to her. Her quite respectable vocabulary was gleaned from these sources and may have equaled Peter's own in size. In addition she possessed an uncanny word sense which helped her greatly in understanding Peter's jargon.

She learned the taste of bananas and frankfurters, chocolate ice cream and Coke, and displayed such an addiction to these delicacies that Peter rapidly put on some of the pounds he had lost. One day she asked him what he looked like.

"Well, I told you I am sixteen, and I'm sort of thin."

"Does thee possess a mirror?" she asked.

"Yes, of course."

At her urging and with some embarrassment he went and stood before a mirrored door in his mother's bedroom.

"Marry," she said after a dubious pause, "I doubt not thee is comely. But folk have changed."

"Now let me look at you," he demanded.

"Nay, we have no mirror."

"Then go and look in the brook. There's a quiet spot below the rock where the water is dark."

He was delighted with her appearance, having remembered Hogarth's unkind representations of a not much later period and being prepared for disappointment. She was in fact very much prettier by Peter's standards than by those of her own time, which favored plumpness and smaller mouths. He told her she was a beauty, and her tentative fondness for him turned instantly to adulation.

Previously Peter had had fleeting glimpses of her slim, smoothly muscled body, as she had bathed or dressed. Now, having seen each other face to face they were overcome by embarrassment and both of them, when not fully clothed, stared resolutely into the corners of the room.

For a time Charity believed that Peter was a dreadful liar. The sight and sound of planes in the sky were not enough to convince her of the fact of flying, so he persuaded his father to take him along on a business flight to Washington. After she had recovered from the marvels of airplane travel, he took her on a walking tour of the Capitol. Now she would believe anything, even that the American Revolution had been a success. They joined his father for lunch at an elegant French restaurant and she experienced, vicariously, the pleasures of half of a half bottle of white wine and a chocolate eclair. Charity was by way of getting spoiled.

Fully recovered and with school only a week away, Peter decided to brush up his tennis. When reading or doing nothing in particular, he was always dimly aware of Charity and her immediate surroundings, and by sharpening his attention he could bring her clearly to the forefront of his mind. Tennis displaced her completely and for an hour or two each day he was unaware of her doings.

Had he been a few years older and a little more knowledgeable and realistic about the world, he might have guessed the peril into which he was leading her. Fictional villainy abounded, of course, and many items in the news didn't bear thinking about, but by his own firsthand experience, people were well intentioned and kindly, and for the most part they reacted to events with reasonable intelligence. It was what he expected instinctively.

A first hint of possible consequences reached him as he walked home from one of his tennis sessions.

"Ursula Miller said an ill thing to me today."

"Oh?" His answer was abstracted since, in all truth, he was beginning to run out of interest in the village gossip which was all the news she had to offer.

"Yesterday she said it was an untruth about the thirteen states. Today she avowed that I was devil ridden. And Ursula has been my best friend."

"I warned you that people wouldn't believe you and you might get yourself laughed at," he said. Then suddenly he caught up in his thinking. "Good Lord—Salem."

"Please, Peter, thee must stop taking thy Maker's name."

"I'll try to remember. Listen, Charity, how many people have you been talking to about our—about what's been happening?"

"As I have said. At first to Father and Aunt Beulah. They did believe I was still addled from the fever."

"And to Ursula."

"Aye, but she vowed to keep it secret."

"Do you believe she will, now that she's started name calling?"

A lengthy pause.

"I fear she may have told the lad who keeps her company."

"I should have warned you. Damn it, I should have laid it on the line."

"Peter!"

"Sorry. Charity, not another word to anybody. Tell Ursula you've been fooling—telling stories to amuse her."

" 'Twould not be right."

"So what. Charity, don't be scared, but listen. People might get to thinking you're a witch."

"Oh, they couldn't."

"Why not?"

"Because I am not one. Witches are—oh, no, Peter." He could sense her growing alarm.

"Go tell Ursula it was a pack of lies. Do it now."

"I must milk the cow."

"Do it now."

"Nay, the cow must be milked."

"Then milk her faster than she's ever been milked before."

On the Sabbath, three little boys threw stones at Charity as she and her father left the church. Obadiah Payne caught one of them and caned him, and then would have had to fight the lad's father save that the pastor intervened.

It was on the Wednesday that calamity befell. Two tight-lipped men approached Obadiah in the fields.

"Squire wants to see thy daughter Charity."

"Squire?"

"Aye. Squire Hacker. He would talk with her at once."

"Squire can talk to me if so be he would have her reprimanded. What has she been up to?"

"Witchcraft, that's what," said the second man, sounding as if he were savoring the dread news. "Croft's old ewe delivered a monstrous lamb. Pointy pinched-up face and an extra eye." He crossed himself.

"Great God!"

" 'Twill do ye no good to blaspheme, Obadiah. She's to come with us now."

"I'll not have it. Charity's no witch, as ye well know, and I'll not have her converse with Squire. Ye mind the Squire's lecherous ways."

"That's not here nor there. Witchcraft is afoot again and all are saying 'tis your Charity at bottom of it."

"She shall not go."

First one, then the other displayed the stout truncheons they had held concealed behind their backs.

" 'Twas of our own good will we told thee first. Come now and instruct thy daughter to go with us featly. Else take a clout on the head and sleep tonight in the gaol house."

They left Obie Payne gripping a broken wrist and staring in numbed bewilderment from his door stoop, and escorted Charity, not touching her, walking at a cautious distance to either side, to Squire Hacker's big house on the hill. In the village proper, little groups of people watched from doorways and, though some had always been her good friends, none had the courage now to speak a word of comfort.

Peter went with her each reluctant step of the way, counting himself responsible for her plight and helpless to do the least thing about it. He sat alone in the living room of his home, eyes closed to sharpen his reading of her surroundings. She offered no response to his whispered reassurances and perhaps did not hear them.

At the door her guards halted and stood aside, leaving her face to face with the grim-visaged squire. He moved backward step by step, and she followed him, as if hypnotized, into the shadowed room.

The squire lowered himself into a high-backed chair. "Look at me."

Unwillingly she raised her head and stared into his face.

Squire Hacker was a man of medium height, very broad in the shoulder and heavily muscled. His face was disfigured by deep pock marks and the scar of a knife cut across the jaw, souvenirs of his earlier years in the Carib Islands. From the Islands he had also brought some wealth which he had since increased manyfold by the buying of land, share cropping and money lending.

"Charity Payne," he said sternly, "take off thy frock."

"No. No, please."

"I command it. Take off thy garments for I must search thee for witch marks."

He leaned forward, seized her arm and pulled her to him. "If thee would avoid public trial and condemnation, thee will do as I say," His hands began to explore her body.

Even by the standards of the time, Charity regularly spent extraordinary hours at hard physical labor and she possessed a strength which would have done credit to many young men. Squire Hacker should have been more cautious.

"Nay," she shouted and drawing back her arm, hit him in the nose with all the force she could muster. He released her with a roar of rage, then, while he was mopping away blood and tears with the sleeve of his ruffled shirt and shouting imprecations, she turned and shot out the door. The guards, converging, nearly grabbed her as she passed but, once she was away, they stood no chance of catching her and for a wonder none of the villagers took up the chase.

She was well on the way home and covering the empty road at a fast trot before Peter was able to gain her attention.

"Charity," he said, "Charity, you mustn't go home. If that s.o.b. of a squire has any influence with the court, you just fixed yourself."

She was beginnning to think again and could even translate Peter's strange language.

"Influence!" she said. "Marry, he is the court. He is the judge."

"Ouch!"

"I wot well I must not be found at home. I am trying to think where to hide. I might have had trial by water. Now they will burn me for a surety. I do remember what folk said about the last witch trials."

"Could you make your way to Boston and then maybe to New York—New Amsterdam?"

"Leave my home forever! Nay. And I would not dare the trip."

"Then take to the woods. Where can you go?"

"Take to—? Oh. To the cave, mayhap."

"Don't too many people know about it?"

"Aye. But there is another across the brook and beyond Tom Carter's freehold. I do believe none know of it but me. 'Tis very small. We must ford the brook just yonder, then walk that fallen tree. There is a trail which at sundown will be tromped by a herd of deer."

"You're thinking about dogs?"

"Aye, on the morrow. There is no good pack in Annes Towne."

"You live in a savage age, Charity."

"Aye," she said wryly. " 'Tis fortunate we have not invented the bomb."

"Damn it," Peter said, "I wish we'd never met. I wish I hadn't taken you on that plane trip. I wish I'd warned you to keep quiet about it."

"Ye could not guess I would be so foolish."

"What can you do out here without food?"

"I'd liefer starve than be in the stocks, but there is food to be had in the forest, some sorts of roots and toadstools and autumn berries. I shall hide myself for three days, I thinks, then seek out my father by night and do as he tells me."

When she was safely hidden in the cave, which was small indeed but well concealed by a thicket of young sassafras, she said:

"Now we can think. First, I would have an answer from thy superior wisdom. Can one be truly a witch and have no knowledge of it?"

"Don't be foolish. There's no such thing as a witch."

"Ah well, 'tis a matter for debate by scholars. I do feel in my heart that I am not a witch, if there be such creatures. That book, Peter, of which ye told me, which recounts the history of these colonies."

"Yes?"

"Will ye look in it and learn if I came to trial and what befell me?"

"There'd be nothing about it. It's just a small book. But—"

To his parents' puzzlement, Peter spent the following morning at the Boston Public Library. In the afternoon he shifted his operations to the Historical Society. He found at last a listing of the names of women known to have been tried for witchcraft between the years 1692 and 1697. Thereafter he could locate only an occasional individual name. There was no record of any Charity Payne in 1700 or later.

He started again when the reading room opened next day, interrupting the task only momentarily for brief exchanges with Charity. His lack of success was cheering to her, for she overestimated the completeness of the records.

At close to noon he was scanning the pages of a photostated doctoral thesis when his eye caught a familiar name.

"Jonas Hacker," it read. "Born Liverpool, England, date uncertain, perhaps 1659, was the principal figure in a curious action of law which has not become a recognized legal precedent in English courts.

"Squire Hacker, a resident of Annes Towne (cf. Anniston), was tried and convicted of willful murder and larceny. The trial was posthumous, several months after his decease from natural causes in 1704. The sentence pronounced was death by hanging which, since it could not be imposed, was commuted to forfeiture of his considerable estate. His land and other possessions reverted to the Crown and were henceforward administered by the Governor of Bay Colony.

"While the motivation and procedure of the court

may have been open to question, evidence of Hacker's guilt was clear cut. The details are these. . . ."

"Hey, Charity," Peter rumbled in his throat.

"Aye?"

"Look at this page. Let me flatten it out."

"Read it please, Peter. Is it bad news?"

"No. Good, I think." He read the paragraphs on Jonas Hacker.

"Oh, Peter, can it be true?"

"It has to be. Can you remember any details?"

"Marry, I remember well when they disappeared, the ship's captain and a common sailor. They were said to have a great sack of gold for some matter of business with Squire. But it could not be, for they never reached his house."

"That's what Hacker said, but the evidence showed that they got there—got there and never got away. Now here's what you must do. Late tonight, go home."

"I would fain do so, for I am terrible athirst."

"No, wait, What's your parson's name?"

"John Hix."

"Can you reach his house tonight without being seen?"

"Aye. It backs on a glen."

"Go there. He can protect you better than your father can until your trial."

"Must I be tried?"

"Of course. We want to clear your name. Now let's do some planning."

The town hall could seat no more than a score of people, and the day was fair; so it was decided that the trial should be held on the common, in discomforting proximity to the stocks.

Visitors came from as far as twenty miles away, afoot or in carts, and nearly filled the common itself. Squire Hacker's own armchair was the only seat provided. Others stood or sat on the patchy grass.

The squire came out of the inn presently, fortified with rum, and took his place. He wore a brocaded coat and a wide-rimmed hat and would have been more impressive if it had not been for his still swollen nose, now permanently askew.

A way was made through the crowd then, and Charity, flanked on one side by John Hix, on the other by his tall son, walked to the place where she was to stand. Voices were suddenly stilled. Squire Hacker did not condescend to look directly at the prisoner, but fixed a cold stare on the minister; a warning that his protection of the girl would not be forgiven. He cleared his throat.

"Charity Payne, is thee willing to swear upon the Book?"

"Aye."

"No mind. We may forgo the swearing. All can see that ye are fearful."

"Nay," John Hix interrupted. "She shall have the opportunity to swear to her word. 'Twould not be legal otherwise." He extended a Bible to Charity, who placed her fingers on it and said, "I do swear to speak naught but the truth."

Squire Hacker glowered and lost no time coming to the attack. "Charity Payne, do ye deny being a witch?"

"I do."

"Ye do be one?"

"Nay, I do deny it."

"Speak what ye mean. What have ye to say of the monstrous lamb born of Master Croft's ewe?"

"I know naught of it."

"Was't the work of Satan?"

"I know not."

"Was't then the work of God?"

"I know not."

"Thee holds then that He might create such a monster?"

"I know naught about it."

"In thy own behalf will thee deny saying that this colony and its neighbors will in due course make war against our King?"

"Nay, I do not deny that."

There was a stir in the crowd and some angry muttering.

"Did ye tell Mistress Ursula Miller that ye had flown a great journey through the air?"

"Nay."

"Mistress Ursula will confound thee in that lie."

"I did tell Ursula that someday folk would travel in that wise. I did tell her that I had seen such travel through eyes other than my own."

Squire Hacker leaned forward. He could not have hoped for a more damning statement. John Hix' head bowed in prayer.

"Continue."

"Aye. I am blessed with a sort of second sight."

"Blessed or cursed?"

"God permits it. It cannot be accursed."

"Continue. What evil things do ye see by this second sight?"

"Most oftentimes I see the world as it will one day be. Thee said evil. Such sights are no more and no less evil than we see around us."

Hacker pondered. There was an uncomfortable wrongness about this child's testimony. She should have been gibbering with fear, when in fact she seemed self-possessed. He wondered if by some strange chance she really had assistance from the devil's minions.

"Charity Payne, thee has confessed to owning second sight. Does thee use this devilish power to spy on thy neighbors?"

It was a telling point. Some among the spectators exchanged discomfited glances.

"Nay, 'tis not devilish, and I cannot see into the doings of my neighbors—except—"

"Speak up, girl. Except what?"

"Once I did perceive by my seeing a most foul murder."

"Murder!" The squire's voice was harsh. A few in the crowd made the sign of the cross.

"Aye. To tell true, two murders. Men whose corpses do now lie buried unshriven in a dark cellar close onto this spot. 'Tween them lies a satchel of golden guineas."

It took a minute for the squire to find his voice.

"A cellar?" he croaked.

"Aye, a root cellar, belike the place one would keep winter apples." She lifted her head and stared straight into the squire's eyes, challenging him to inquire further.

The silence was ponderous as he strove to straighten out his thoughts. To this moment he was safe, for her words described every cellar in and about the village. But she knew. Beyond any question, she knew. Her gaze, seeming to penetrate the darkest corners of his mind, told him that, even more clearly than her words.

Squire Hacker believed in witches and considered them evil and deserving of being destroyed. He had seen and shuddered at the horrible travesty of a lamb in farmer Croft's stable yard, but he had seen like deformities in the Caribbee and did not hold the event an evidence of witchcraft. Not for a minute had he thought Charity a witch, for she showed none of the signs. Her wild talk and the growing rumors had simply seemed to provide the opportunity for some dalliance with a pretty young girl and possibly, in exchange for an acquittal, a lien upon her father's land.

Now he was unsure. She must indeed have second sight to have penetrated his secret, for it had been stormy that night five years ago, and none had seen the missing sailors near to his house. Of that he was confident. Further, shockingly, she knew how and where they lay buried. Another question and answer could not be risked.

He moved his head slowly and looked right and left at the silent throng.

"Charity Payne," he said, picking his words with greatest care, "has put her hand on the Book and sworn to tell true, an act, I opine, she could scarce perform, were she a witch. Does any person differ with me?"

John Hix looked up in startled hopefulness.

"Very well. The lambing at Master Croft's did have the taint of witchcraft, but Master Trowbridge has stated his belief that some noxious plant is growing in Croft's pasture, and 'tis at the least possible. Besides, the ewe is old and she has thrown runty lambs before.

"To quote Master Trowbridge again, he holds that

the cholera which has afflicted us so sorely comes from naught but the drinking of bad water. He advises boiling it. I prefer adding a little rum."

He got the laughter he sought. There was a lessening of tension.

"As to second sight." Again he swept the crowd with his gaze. "Charity had laid claim to it, and I called it a devilish gift to test her, but second sight is not witchcraft, as ye well know. My own grandmother had it, and a better woman ne'er lived. I hold it to be a gift of God. Would any challenge me?

"Very well. I would warn Charity to be cautious in what she sees and tells, for second sight can lead to grievous disputations. I do not hold with her story of two murdered men although I think that in her own sight she is telling true. If any have aught of knowledge of so dire a crime, I adjure him to step forth and speak."

He waited. "Nobody? Then, by the authority conferred on me by his Excellency the Governor, I declare that Charity Payne is innocent of the charges brought. She may be released."

This was not at all the eventuality which a few of Squire Hacker's cronies had foretold. The crowd had clearly expected a day-long inquisition climaxed by a prisoner to bedevil in the stocks. The Squire's aboutface and his abrupt ending of the trial surprised them and angered a few. They stood uncertain.

Then someone shouted hurrah and someone else called for three cheers for Squire Hacker, and all in a minute the gathering had lost its hate and was taking on the look of a picnic. Men headed for the tavern. Parson Hix said a long prayer to which few listened, and everybody gathered around to wring Obie Payne's good hand and to give his daughter a squeeze.

At intervals through the afternoon and evening Peter touched lightly on Charity's mind, finding her carefree and happily occupied with visitors. He chose not to obtrude himself until she called.

Late that night she lay on her mattress and stared into the dark.

"Peter," she whispered.

"Yes, Charity."

"Oh, thank you again."

"Forget it. I got you into the mess. Now you're out of it. Anyway, I didn't really help. It all had to work out the way it did, because that's the way it had happened. You see?"

"No, not truly. How do we know that Squire won't dig up those old bones and burn them?"

"Because he didn't. Four years from now somebody will find them."

"No, Peter, I do not understand, and I am afeared again."

"Why, Charity?"

"It must be wrong, thee and me talking together

like this and knowing what is to be and what is not."

"But what could be wrong about it?"

"That I do not know, but I think 'twere better you should stay in your time and me in mine. Good-bye, Peter."

"Charity!"

"And God bless you."

Abruptly she was gone and in Peter's mind there was an emptiness and a knowledge of being alone. He had not known that she could close him out like this.

With the passing of days he became skeptical and in time he might have disbelieved entirely. But Charity visited him again. It was October. He was alone and studying, without much interest.

"Peter."

"Charity, it's you."

"Yes. For a minute, please Peter, for only a minute, but I had to tell you. I —" She seemed somehow embarrassed. "There is a message."

"A what?"

"Look at Bear Rock, Peter, under the bear's jaw on the left side."

With that, she was gone.

The cold water swirled around his legs as he traced with one finger the painstakingly chiseled message she had left; a little-girl message in a symbol far older than either of them.

Mary Cary

The Entrance Exam

If at first you don't succeed,
just keep plaguing them.

Kate Fotheringay sat in the office of the headmistress of Miss Perkle's School for Young Gentlewomen. She sat in the third largest chair. The headmistress, Miss Perkle herself, sat behind a huge and dusty desk in a chair that was almost a throne. This, thought Kate, was only proper. A headmistress was a headmistress, and Miss Perkle was a very old lady who had earned the right to the biggest chair.

She was indeed old, though how old no one knew. Kate wondered for a moment whether she might once have lived in a castle way back in the Middle Ages. Perhaps she had seen the fall of the Roman Empire. Or watched as the first stones were laid for the Tower of London. Had she really come to America on the

Mayflower, as Kate's mother said? Had she really been at Salem when the witches were hung?

No matter. She was a lovely old lady with dandelion-white hair and wrinkled, pink cheeks. Her office was lovely, too. A black cat snoozed in a basket near the file cabinet. A stuffed monkey sat on top of the book-case. There was a crystal ball on the windowsill and a hollowed-out skull on the desk. The skull contained Miss Perkle's supply of paper clips.

The school was wonderful beyond Kate's dreams.

Kate and her mother had driven out from town on Cemetery Road. It was a narrow, twisting lane that wound through a grove of oak trees. Then it passed the old graveyard where headstones leaned toward each other as if they were whispering secrets. Across from the cemetery was the school, a soot-stained, ivy-covered stone building. It smelled of age and cobwebs and dust, with just a faint hint of mice.

Kate and her mother had waited in the ebony parlor until Miss Perkle could see them. Even the walls in the parlor were black, and the heavy curtains were drawn so that not the tiniest ray of sunlight could enter. A single candle burned on the table, and in the gloom Kate could barely see the pictures on the walls. They were all portraits of women. Kate knew that most of them were very old. She also knew that all of the women had been witches.

It wasn't known in the town, of course, but all graduates of Miss Perkle's School were witches. Kate's mother was a witch. And Kate would be a witch, too. Miss Perkle would see to it. The townspeople only knew that Miss Perkle's School was very, very private and that not many girls were admitted. But Kate knew that witchcraft was what Miss Perkle and her very private school were all about.

When at last Kate and her mother had been summoned from the gloom of the ebony parlor, Kate sat in Miss Perkle's office and watched Miss Perkle open a big book with parchment pages. "How old is the child?" Miss Perkle asked. Her voice was like the rustle of dry leaves.

"Almost ten," said Kate's mother.

"Excellent," said Miss Perkle. She wrote it down with a quill pen. Then she stared at Kate through her square, old-fashioned glasses. "You look clever enough," she said. "Are you clever, Katherine?"

"Yes, Miss Perkle," said Kate. She wasn't bragging. It was the simple truth. Kate was at the head of her class. She knew arithmetic and astronomy and English literature and ancient history and lots of other things besides.

Her mother handed an envelope to Miss Perkle. "Here are Kate's records from the public school," she said. "I've saved all her report cards."

Miss Perkle tumbled the cards out onto her desk.

She glanced at them and nodded. Then she wrote again in her big book. The quill pen scratched nicely. Kate liked the sound. The principal at the public school wrote with a ball-point that didn't make any noise at all.

"So far so good," said Miss Perkle. "Now there is a matter of the entrance examination. As you know, Miss Perkle's School is an unusual one. We cannot rely on ordinary records or on ordinary accomplishments. Katherine must have at least a smattering of Greek. Some fine spells come to us from the Greeks. And she should know Latin. Several of our courses are given entirely in Latin."

"She'll pass the exam," said Kate's mother. "I've been tutoring her at home."

"Very well," said Miss Perkle. "We will schedule the examination for her birthday. When is her birthday?"

Kate's mother paused. "It's . . . it's sometime next month. About the fifteenth, I think."

"You think?" echoed Miss Perkle. She laid her quill pen down and looked sternly at Mrs. Fotheringay. "Surely you know your own child's birthday."

"Not . . . not precisely," said Kate's mother.

"Abigail Constance Murdock Fotheringay!" cried Miss Perkle. When she used all of Kate's mother's names, she sounded quite threatening. "You were a brilliant student. Has your brain turned to oatmeal? You cannot have forgotten the day Katherine was born!"

Mrs. Fotheringay looked down at her own hands.

"I wasn't there the day she was born," she said, very softly. "Miss Perkle, Kate is truly gifted. I know the rule that—"

Miss Perkle interrupted. "That all young ladies admitted to the school are the daughters of graduates, or at very least their granddaughters. Are you telling me that Katherine is *not* your daughter?"

"But she *is* my daughter!" cried Mrs. Fotheringay. "I took her in when she was a tiny baby. I raised her and loved her. If I'm not her mother, who is?"

"I am sure I do not know," said Miss Perkle. She stood up and shut her big book with a clap. "Katherine is not related to you by blood. We accept only those whose mothers or grandmothers have studied with us. A rule is a rule, and we make no exceptions."

"Miss Perkle, please," said Kate's mother.

"Adoption does not count!" snapped Miss Perkle.

Kate decided that Miss Perkle was not a pretty old lady after all. Kate wished she could turn Miss Perkle into a toadstool—an ugly, yellow toadstool with red speckles.

"Don't be silly, child," snapped Miss Perkle, although Kate hadn't said a word. "You cannot turn me into a toadstool. You are not a witch. You are only an ordinary little girl who makes good marks in school."

Suddenly the door banged open and a plump, round-faced woman bounced into the office. She was completely out of breath. "Miss Perkle!" The newcomer waved a folded newspaper. "The most terrible thing! On the second page! The paper just came!"

Miss Perkle took the newspaper and opened it. After she read for a moment, her pink, wrinkled cheeks turned ashy white. She looked up from the paper and her eyes were wide and staring.

"Miss Perkle?" said Kate's mother. "What is it?"

Miss Perkle folded the newspaper and put it down on her desk. "The mayor wishes to straighten and widen Cemetery Road," she said. "He intends to ask the town council to condemn our property and tear down our school to make way for this project."

"Oh, no!" cried Kate's mother.

"Please excuse me, Abigail," said Miss Perkle. "I must go and see the mayor."

"But Miss Perkle, about Kate . . ."

Miss Perkle shook her head. "We will not discuss the matter further. I have important things to do. I am going into town now."

She did go, leaving Mrs. Fotheringay and Kate in the office.

They drove slowly home along the narrow, twisting road. Mrs. Fotheringay did not talk. Kate cried.

There was another story in the newspaper the next day. It said the mayor wanted Miss Perkle to be paid for her property. It said she could move her school into a new building nearer town. There was a picture above the story showing the mayor sitting behind his desk. He was smiling. At least, he was trying to smile.

"He's got lots of warts," said Kate to her mother.

"I can guess how he got them," said Mrs. Fotheringay. "Miss Perkle was always very good at warts. But it looks as if a few warts aren't going to save the school. Sounds as if the mayor's sticking to his guns."

The next week the members of the town council voted. They approved the new road. They condemned Miss Perkle's School. No sooner had the councilmen voted than one of them came down with chicken pox, in spite of the fact that he had had chicken pox once before. Another council member fell down his cellar stairs and fractured his arm in two places. Soon after that, a third councilman ran out of his house at midnight, screaming that the place was suddenly full of bats.

"Miss Perkle and her teachers are doing their worst," said Mrs. Fotheringay.

But the worst was not bad enough. The council did not change its vote and the mayor did not change his mind.

"Maybe Miss Perkle will like a new building," said Kate.

Her mother sighed. "It would never be the same. Everyone who ever went to Miss Perkle's loves the place.

"Kate, do you know that some of the cobwebs there

are two hundred years old? And there are toadstools in the basement and wolfbane in the herb garden out back. It would take years to replace those cobwebs and grow new toadstools. It would take centuries!"

"Well, they won't let me in anyway, so who cares?" said Kate.

But Kate did care. She cared enough to be there with her mother when the bulldozers appeared on Cemetery Road. There was to be quite a fuss about fixing the road. The mayor himself was to dig the first spadeful of earth before the bulldozers started tearing up the old roadway to make way for the new.

The members of the town council came for the ceremony. One of them had bright-green hair, and quite naturally he kept his hat on. The newspaper reporters were there and so was a crew from the television station. Some townspeople were there, and so was each and every teacher and student from Miss Perkle's School. Miss Perkle held her head high, but her lips trembled and her eyes were red. She had been weeping.

A brass band took its place before the bulldozers and played a brave tune. The television camera focused on the mayor. The mayor bent, and the spade in his extremely warty hand touched the stony surface of the old road.

Suddenly Kate found herself wriggling through the

crowd. In a second she was past the members of the town council and the television crew and the newspapermen. She was beside the mayor.

He smiled a false smile at her. "Out of the way, little girl," he said.

Kate said something—no one heard quite what— and she made a little motion with her hand. Then she turned and walked back through the crowd, back to her mother's side.

The mayor bent again to his digging. His spade broke through the rutted surface. And suddenly, from that break, something green appeared—something green and thorny that grew and grew and grew.

The mayor shouted and leaped backward as the prickly vine caught at his clothes.

The television crew retreated hastily, taking their camera down the road. A long way down the road.

A burly operator who had been waiting on his bulldozer stared for a moment at the giant briar that now blocked the roadway, then he shouted, "Hey! What the heck?" and his machine roared and rumbled at the magical plant.

An instant later the vine had surrounded the machine. It seemed to gobble it up. The bulldozer operator ran for his life.

And so did the mayor.

And the councilmen.

So did the newspapermen and the townspeople.

So did everyone except Miss Perkle and her teachers and students. And of course Kate and her mother.

"They won't widen the road," said Kate to Miss Perkle. "And they won't tear down the school, either."

She made another motion with her hand and the spiny, thorny, prickly vine withered and shriveled and dried up and blew away, leaving the road empty except for the bulldozers.

Miss Perkle looked extremely alarmed.

"Don't worry," said Kate. "The vine will grow again any time they try to work on the road."

"My dear child," said Miss Perkle, "how on earth do you do that? All of us excel at causing warts and summoning bats and making things fall down or fly up, but never, not since the days of the famous witch Hephzibah Carew, have we been able to cause the magic thorn tree to grow. Where did you learn that marvelous spell?"

"I'm not sure," said Kate. "I think I heard it once in a dream."

They all walked back then, along the narrow, twisting old road to the school. And Miss Perkle and Kate and her mother had tea in the ebony parlor, where the portraits of the famous old graduates looked down from their frames and the drapes were drawn against the sun and a single candle burned on the table.

"Kate does have power, you see," said Kate's mother. "I tried to tell you. Even if she is a foundling and we don't know who her real mother is, she has power."

"A foundling?" said Miss Perkle.

"Left on my doorstep," admitted Kate's mother. "She was only a tiny thing. But she has power, even if she isn't descended from a graduate."

Miss Perkle looked puzzled. Could an ordinary child be a real witch? Then Miss Perkle looked over her shoulder at one of the dim old pictures that hung on the dark wall. And Miss Perkle took the candle from the table and held it up next to the picture. She looked at the painted face and the painted face looked back at her. It was like looking at a picture of Kate. The girl in the painting was older, of course, but unmistakably like Kate.

"Of course," said Miss Perkle. "I should have noticed. Kate is *not* an ordinary child. She is without any doubt the descendant of Hephzibah Carew, our most brilliant graduate. The resemblance is striking, and she does have the power."

"Not always," admitted Kate. "Once the Phelps kid swiped my roller skates and I tried to turn him into a frog. It didn't work."

"No?" said Miss Perkle.

"No. He turned into a bumblebee and stung me."

"Never mind." Miss Perkle put the candle back on the table. "You're young. Wait until you've finished your education and are a proper witch with a proper diploma."

"Then you'll take me?" cried Kate.

"You may begin classes on Monday," said Miss Perkle.

Kate looked happily around the ebony walls. She thought of the collection of antique cobwebs, and the herb garden with its wolfbane, and the cellar jammed with delightful toadstools. Then she thought of something else.

"What about the entrance exam?" she asked.

"Dear Katherine," said Miss Perkle. "Do not worry your head about an entrance exam. You have already passed it."

Lafcadio Hearn

The Boy Who Drew Cats

*This young artist found that
"Practice makes purrfect."*

A long, long time ago, in a small country village in Japan, there lived a poor farmer and his wife, who were very good people. They had a number of children, and found it hard to feed them all. The elder son was strong enough when only fourteen years old to help his father; and the little girls learned to help their mother almost as soon as they could walk.

But the youngest child, a little boy, did not seem to be fit for hard work. He was very clever—cleverer than all his brothers and sisters; but he was quite weak and small, and people said he could never grow very big. So his parents thought it would be better for him to become a priest than to become a farmer. They took him with them to the village temple one day, and asked the good old priest who lived there if he would have their little boy for his pupil, and teach him all that a priest ought to know.

The old man spoke kindly to the lad, and asked him some hard questions. So clever were the answers that the priest agreed to take the little fellow into the temple as an acolyte, and to educate him for the priesthood.

The boy learned quickly what the old priest taught him, and was very obedient in most things. But he had one fault. He liked to draw cats during study hours, and to draw cats when cats ought not to have been drawn at all.

Whenever he found himself alone, he drew cats. He drew them on the margins of the priest's books, and on all the screens of the temple, on the walls, and on the pillars. Several times the priest told him this was not right; but he did not stop drawing cats. He drew them because he could not really help it. He had what is called "the genius of an artist," and just for that reason he was not quite fit to be an acolyte; a good acolyte should study books.

One day after he had drawn some very clever pictures of cats upon a paper screen, the old priest said· to him severely, "My boy, you must go away from this temple at once. You will never make a good priest, but perhaps you will become a great artist. Now let me give you a last piece of advice, and be sure you never forget it. *Avoid large places at night; keep to small!*"

The boy did not know what the priest meant by saying, "*Avoid large places; keep to small!*" He thought and thought, while he was tying up his little bundle of clothes to go away; but he could not understand those words, and he was afraid to speak to the priest anymore, except to say good-bye.

He left the temple very sorrowfully, and began to wonder what he should do. If he went straight home he felt his father would punish him for having been disobedient to the priest: so he was afraid to go home. All at once he remembered that at the next village, twelve miles away, there was a very big temple. He had heard there were several priests at that temple; and he made up his mind to go to them and ask them to take him for their acolyte.

Now that big temple was closed up but the boy did not know this fact. The reason it had been closed up was that a goblin had frightened the priests away, and had taken possession of the place. Some brave warriors had afterwards gone to the temple at night to kill the goblin; but they had never been seen alive again. Nobody had ever told these things to the boy; so he walked all the way to the village hoping to be kindly treated by the priests.

When he got to the village it was already dark, and

all the people were in bed; but he saw the big temple
on a hill on the other end of the principal street, and
he saw there was a light in the temple. People who
tell the story say the goblins used to make that light,
in order to tempt lonely travelers to ask for shelter.
The boy went at once to the temple, and knocked.
There was no sound inside. He knocked and knocked
again; but still nobody came. At last he pushed gently
at the door, and was glad to find that it had not been
fastened. So he went in and saw a lamp burning—but
no priest.

He thought that some priest would be sure to come
very soon, and he sat down and waited. Then he noticed that everything in the temple was gray with dust,
and thickly spun over with cobwebs. So he thought to
himself that the priests would certainly like to have
an acolyte, to keep the place clean. He wondered why
they had allowed the place to get so dusty. What most
pleased him, however, were some big white screens,
good to paint cats upon. Though he was tired, he looked
at once for a writing box and found one, and ground
some ink, and began to paint cats.

He painted a great many cats upon the screens; and
then he began to feel very, very sleepy. He was just
on the point of lying down to sleep beside one of the
screens, when he suddenly remembered the words:
"*Avoid large places—keep to small!*"

The temple was very large; he was alone; and as he

thought of these words—though he could not quite understand them—he began to feel for the first time a little afraid; and he resolved to look for a small place in which to sleep. He found a little cabinet, with a sliding door, and went into it and shut himself up. Then he lay down and fell fast asleep.

Very late in the night he was awakened by a most terrible noise—a noise of fighting and screaming. It was so dreadful that he was afraid even to look through a chink of the little cabinet; he lay very still, holding his breath for fright.

The light that had been in the temple went out; but the awful sounds continued, and became more awful, and all the temple shook. After a long time silence came; but the boy was still afraid to move. He did not move until the light of the morning sun shone into the cabinet through the chinks of the little door.

Then he got out of his hiding place very cautiously, and looked about. The first thing he saw was that all the floor of the temple was covered with blood. And then he saw, lying dead in the middle of it, an enormous monstrous rat—a goblin rat—bigger than a cow!

But who or what could have killed it? There was no man or other creature to be seen. Suddenly the boy observed that the mouths of all the cats he had drawn the night before were red and wet with blood. Then he new that the goblin had been killed by the cats which he had drawn. And then also, for the first time, he understood why the wise old priest had said to him:—*"Avoid large places at night; keep to small."*

Afterwards that boy became a very famous artist. Some of the cats which he drew are still shown to travelers in Japan.